MW01716471

# How To Save a Billionaire

# - Free Love Story -

CASSIE Hillsdale isn't looking for love. She's just looking to survive the bank robbery she finds herself in the middle of!

*Roses and Robberies*, a short suspensful love story, is available for free! Visit Izi Miller's website or scan the QR code below to get your copy!

For my readers -
you made my dream come true


Published in the United States by Village Lane Publishing.

Visit us on the web!
www.VillageLanePublishing.com

Printed in the United States of America
First Edition

graduated high school and I still feel like a lunch-table outcast.

I should have gotten myself a fake boyfriend for this reunion like in those romance movies. And then we would fall in love for real. And life would be great.

I snort.

"Amy?"

I turn in my chair. "Kathryn?"

"Oh my goodness! Amy! How are you?" She holds out her arms to embrace me.

I stand up, more out of social obligation than wanting to hug her. We weren't close in high school and haven't spoken once since. Not even on social media. But she hugs me to her like we're long lost sisters. She was like this in high school too, treating everyone like they were her bosom buddies. At least for a moment.

"Oh, Amy! It's been so long! How are you?"

Her little black top and white skirt are accented with gold heels and gold hoop earrings. She looks even more beautiful than she did in high school, and she was the beauty queen back then. I self-consciously tug at my jeans. At least I wore a nice shirt. I think it's the type of top people like Kathryn would call a blouse. But that's just a guess. I was tempted to wear a comfy t-shirt and hoodie, but I figured I should at least try to look like a grown up.

"Doing great," I say, injecting false enthusiasm into my

# How To Save a Billionaire

- A SWEET SUSPENSE NOVEL -

IZI MILLER

voice. "How are you?"

"Todd, this is Amy," Kathryn says to the man she's with.

He smiles in a distant but polite way. None of Kathryn's false enthusiasm has rubbed off on him.

"It's actually Amy-Kate," I say.

"Amy, this is my husband Todd." Kathryn tousles his hair like he's five. His polite smile doesn't falter, and I have to give him credit for taking that like a champ.

"Nice to meet you, Amy," he says, holding out a hand for me to shake.

"Nice to meet you too. You know-"

"Oh look!" says Kathryn. "There's Margaret! You simply have to meet her!" She tugs Todd away who at least has the decency to wave as he's dragged off.

I slump back down at my table and pick at the confetti on the tabletop. Why am I here? This was a terrible idea! I sigh, wondering if I should give up on this whole socializing thing and call it a day. I'd had some vague notion of this high school reunion being fun, of me showing up looking all cute and like I had my life under control. Did I want those girls that had made fun of me in high school to be jealous of me? Maybe a little. Was that petty of me? Very.

"Oh, look who it is."

I cringe. I know that voice. Turning slowly, I plaster on a smile. "Hey, Amanda."

She and her two best friends stand shoulder to shoulder,

facing me. It's like the high school hallways all over again.

She smiles, close lipped and flat-eyed. "So nice to see you. What are you up to these days?"

I straighten my shoulders and try to look confident. Amanda was the girl everyone wanted to impress in high school — prom queen and supreme clique leader. It's like some reflex, apparently, to want to impress her. This is the moment I may have let myself daydream about for a second while getting dressed for the reunion. The moment when I wow Amanda with my life successes. Where she exclaims over my adorable outfit and says how jealous she is of my job. "Just working for Isomo." Like working for the biggest tech company in the world is no big deal.

"Wow!" said one of her friends. "That's really cool!"

Amanda only raises an eyebrow. "What do you do for them?"

Dang it. I try to hedge. "Oh, this and that." I wave my hand. "It's such a great company!"

"I see."

I deflate. I'm sure she does. This is so not going the way I had envisioned. I can't hide the mess of my life behind a cute outfit.

"What are you up to?" I ask, even though I already know the answer.

She smiles, predatory-like. "You haven't heard?"

"Her make-up company is just the biggest thing out

there!" says her friend on the left. Lola, or Layla or something.

Amanda tosses her hair. "Oh, you flatter me. I mean, it is used by celebrities and such, and we pride ourselves on using only organic, cruelty-free, non-GMO, responsibly-sourced materials. But there is always-" She looks down her nose at me. "-room for improvement."

I get the feeling I'm the one who needs the improvement.

"Wow. That's so cool. You must be really proud of what you've accomplished."

"Oh, of course! Everyone should feel like they're contributing and making a difference in the world. Oh, and here's Brad. You know him, of course."

Brad puts his arm around Amanda's waist and grins at me. He's handsome in a classical way - big and strong with a chiseled chin and blond hair. He looks vaguely familiar, but I'm not sure why. He must have been on the football team or something in high school. I wasn't really into sports.

"Pleased to meet you," I say, holding out my hand for him to shake. His hand swallows mine whole and I worry I won't recover it in one piece as he squeezes and shakes, grinning.

Finally, I manage to free my hand and quickly tuck it into my arm pit, folding my arms.

"Brad's had a great week, haven't you honey?" she says, making goo-goo eyes at him. I want to gag.

He nods.

"He just made the news - innovative football coach leading team to victory. I'm sure you saw it. It was all over the news."

I stretch my lips into a smile and don't reply.

"Oh, that's right," she says. "You aren't into sports are you?" She makes a pouting face. "That must be hard, not having such quality entertainment."

"It's really not that hard at all," I say. "There are other things I like doing like-"

"Speaking of the news," she says. "That whole story about those dead millionaires is so disturbing. I was just telling Brad the other day, I was saying, what is this world coming to? I do my best to make the world a better place, but there is only so much each of us can do. One person can make the world so much worse for everyone in it. It's just tragic."

"Tragic," echoes Layla or Lala.

I don't reply. This is exactly why I don't watch the news. Too depressing.

"Oh! In other exciting news, have you heard?" Amanda holds out her left hand to show me a gigantic glittering diamond ring.

"Oh! Congratulations." I say. "When is the big day?"

"We haven't picked a date yet," she says, admiring the ring, tilting her hand to let it catch the light. "But we're thinking next spring."

"Wonderful." Of course she has a handsome fiance. Of course she's getting married. Of course she owns a successful celebrity makeup company. And I'd thought this evening couldn't get any worse.

"So." Amanda's eyes narrow. "Are you dating anyone?"

I swallow.

# Chapter Two

"AMY-KATE!"

I turn to see a wonderfully familiar guy with curly brown hair and glasses.

"Fred! You made it!"

"Oh look. It's little Freddie," says Amanda to her hench-girls.

Fred nods his head in their direction. He's over six feet tall, towering over my petite 5'5" frame, with broad shoulders. His hair is the same as always - a brown floof of curls on top of his head. He's dressed the same as he always is too - t-shirt and jeans. I guess he didn't feel the need to dress up tonight like I did. The t-shirt has a drawing of a cute cat in a cardboard box with the word "Schrodinger" scrawled on it in sharpie. It's a physics joke.

As I see Amanda sizing him up, I remember how Fred looked in high school. He used to be scrawny, and shorter than most of the girls with out-of-control acne. A lot has changed. A lot has changed for all of us.

I expect Amanda to say something negative about him. If anyone can find flaws even in the best people, it's Amanda.

"You've grown," she finally says.

Fred laughs. "So everyone keeps telling me! I just thought the rest of you got smaller!"

I laugh.

"What are you doing for work then?" Amanda asks, folding her arms and stepping forward. I sense danger.

Fred grins, completely un-intimidated. "This!" He points to his t-shirt.

Amanda frowns. "Putting cats in boxes?"

Fred laughs. "That would be awesome! Cats loves boxes! But no. I've got my own graphic design company," he says, a note of pride in his voice. I remember high school again and how he was always doodling.

Amanda looks surprised.

Fred produces a business card from his back pocket, presenting it to Amanda with a flourish. "We make t-shirts."

Amanda's surprise morphs into a smirk as she takes the card. I can see a picture of a chemistry beaker with four cute little moles stuffed into it. Like the animal, not the measurement. Underneath the picture it says, "four moles per liter."

To the right of the picture is the logo for "Ner-tees" in a cool font and then in smaller letters underneath: "Not your science professor's t-shirts."

His cards are so nerdy. It's awesome.

"T-shirts," she says. "That's cute."

Behind her, her two friends snicker. I kind of want to punch them.

"Is the punch good?" Fred asks me, nodding at my half-full cup on the table, apparently oblivious to Amanda's snub.

I shrug. "As long as your expectations are pretty low, than yeah. It's good."

He nods. "I'll have a glass then. No one's spiked it, right?" He grins. "Have a good day, Amanda! Come on, Amy-Kate!" Fred waves for me to follow him over to the refreshment table where he ladles punch into a plastic cup.

I glance back to wave at Amanda and see her watching the two of us with disdain. It probably looks like we're dating, which is fine, especially tonight where not having a boyfriend seems equal to life failure. Fred is great as a friend. But he's not exactly the type of guy I'm looking to actually date. He's just so… Fred.

Punch in hand, he leads me back to our table that is now Amanda-free and settles his tall frame into a plastic stackable chair. I take the chair two seats over from him, trying to make it obvious to anyone watching that we are not an item. Just friends. Like in high school. Well, actually everyone thought we were dating then too. Dang it.

"Rachelle can't make it?" Fred asks.

I shake my head. "It's too late at night. The baby's already asleep."

He nods. Rachelle was the third member of our little gang in high school. Unlike the two of us, she got snatched up by a rich handsome husband a couple years after graduation and now has an adorable chubby six-month-old girl named Fiona.

"So," he says, leaning back in his chair and stretching his long legs under the table. "Amy-Kate, what have you been up to for the past ten years?"

I laugh. "You, of all people, know exactly what I've been up to!"

"Pretend I don't. Pretend we're just meeting for the first time since high school." He leans forward, resting his elbows on the table and smiles. "Amy-Kate! I was hoping you'd be here! Long time no see!"

I laugh. "Wow. Yeah. So long." We hung out yesterday.

"Tell me all about your life!"

"All about it?"

"Don't worry about it taking too long. We have all night," he says, and sips his punch. He makes a face. "You said this was good!"

"I said it was good if your expectations were low."

"Apparently they weren't low enough." He pushes the cup away from him.

"There really isn't much too tell." I flop back in the chair.

"That's not true!"

"No, for real! I'm trying to wrack my brain for anything interesting. My life right now consists of sitting at a desk, answering a phone, and occasionally getting to arrange flowers."

"Your mom still has that flower shop?"

"Yup." The flower shop was where we ate tacos yesterday.

"Ah," he says, leaning back. "I remember those good old days when we would hang out at that shop after school. That was where I bought a corsage and boutonniere for prom!"

I laugh. "I forgot about that! We made the corsages ourselves, didn't we?"

"Yeah, and mine turned out terrible!" He laughs. "And you were nice enough to swap with me so then you had to give your date this mangled corsage with all the flowers falling out!"

I laugh. "It wasn't that bad!"

"Oh, it was."

"Who did you go with anyway? I can't remember."

"Beatrice," he says, and looks around. "Where is she anyway?"

I shrug and glance around too. "I haven't seen her tonight. Last I heard she lived in Washington and had three kids."

"Way to go, Beatrice!"

"Jealous?" I tease.

He laughs. "Naw. She was just a friend. Neither of us had

dates and we were both in the astronomy club, so we decided to go together." He sighs. "Oh, the good old days."

I snort, almost spilling punch. "You think of high school fondly?"

"Of course! Don't you? I thought everyone came to these things to relive the glory days." He winks. "Naw, in all seriousness, high school was good for its time, but I'm glad those days are over."

"Amen!" I raised my punch glass and we clinked plastic cups together.

"So how is work going?" he asks.

I cringe. "Oh, you know." I wave my hand. "Fine."

"You still hate it, don't you?"

I shrug. "It pays the bills."

"I'm telling you, you should just quit."

"And do what?"

"Help your mom with the flower shop," he says like it's the most obvious thing in the world.

I shake my head. "So what about you? Since we haven't seen each other in ten years," I say sarcastically, "What are you up to in life? I heard you have a t-shirt company?"

He grins. "Oh, yeah! I design them all myself! This is one of them!" He points again at the shirt he's wearing.

"That's cool."

"It glows in the dark! Only the glow in the dark cat is dead! Get it?"

I laugh. "That must be one of your new ones. I haven't seen it before. Business is going well then?" It always boggles my mind how well his company is doing. Like, really. How many people could possibly want glow in the dark dead cat shirts? Don't get me wrong. His shirts are awesome! I just never realized how big the market is for nerdy shirts.

Fred nods making his hair bounce. "It's awesome! Oh, I don't think I told you yet. We just signed the contract to start printing at the bigger printing place!"

"Oh, that's awesome! It's so cool you get to do something you love!"

He's grinning so broad that his energy is infectious. "I know, right?"

The conversation lulls and he takes a sip of punch, then makes a face. "Even knowing it's going to be bad, it's still gross. Please, take this so I don't accidentally drink it again!" He slides the cup over to me. "But enough about me. Are you dating anyone?" He waggles his eyebrows at me.

"Ugh. Do we have to talk about that? Seriously, you're taking this whole pretend scenario a little far."

"Okay, okay," he says. "Just making sure you're free this Friday."

"Valentine's Day?"

He picks up some of the confetti on the table and lets it fall, glittering, back to the plastic table cloth. "It's not Valentine's Day when you don't have a significant other. It's just Singles Awareness Day."

"Fair enough."

"Want to go to dinner that night?"

"Dinner?" We hang out all the time. We even grab lunch occasionally when we get hungry. But a planned dinner? On Valentine's Day? Is this a date? Fred is still playing with the confetti and won't meet my eyes. If I didn't know any better, I'd say he was blushing a little.

But this can't be a date. Because this is Fred. We're just friends.

I debate for a moment. Part of me is hoping that my ex, Evan, will call and say he's sorry and make it up to me with a sweepingly romantic dinner that night. Another part hopes Evan will fall off the bridge over the river that runs through town and I'll never hear from him again, and instead I'll meet some handsome stranger and get swept into a whirlwind romance before this Friday. Most of me realizes these are all highly unlikely.

So I shrug and say, "All right. I guess we can hang out." Because that is all this will be. Hanging out. As friends. Just like normal.

"Awesome!" He finally looks up and smiles at me, like this is the best news he's had all day.

That makes me slightly nervous, but I smile too. Hanging out with Fred is always fun. And anything will be better than sitting at home alone.

# Chapter Three

I FIRST SEE my dream man on Friday morning.

He's tall, with wavy chocolate hair and light cinnamon skin. I lick my lips as the line at the coffee shop moves forward.

His eyes are as warm and brown as hot chocolate, and I just want to eat him up. Okay, maybe I'm a little hungry. But whoever this guy is, he is yummy looking!

He's standing to the side of the line, presumably waiting for his order to be ready, along with a few other people who look like poor mortals beside his god-like features. He's dressed in a navy business suit, but with no tie and the top two buttons left undone on his white shirt. His hair is close cut on the sides and a little longer on top. He looks like he might have been a swimmer in his high school days, lean and toned. His cheekbones would make any girl envious, but his strong jaw makes him look sturdy and masculine.

A woman behind me touches my shoulder and I realize the line has moved forward without me. I give the woman a quick smile and step forward.

This is my favorite coffee shop and it's always busy, but with it being a holiday that celebrates chocolate and love and all that, it's extra busy. The delicious man is looking at a display of little heart shaped chocolates done up in small cellophane bags with curling ribbon. A chalk sign beside them says, "Say it with chocolate!"

I'm not a fan of this particular holiday. It doesn't even have the decency to give me the day off work like real holidays. And after two consecutive years of gaining boyfriends in the spring (after Valentine's Day) and then losing them in the winter (before Valentines Day), I've spent enough time eating heart shaped chocolates alone to resent the pink and red cheer.

He doesn't have a wedding ring on. That's a pleasant sign. Frowning, he turns his attention to a pyramid of white mugs with red cursive on them saying, "I Love You a Latte." He lifts one of the mugs, turning it upside down to read the price tag. His frown deepens and he sets it back down. Even his frown is adorable, making a dip in his skin between his eyebrows. His lips are pursed slightly as he continues to contemplate the display, as if he's deep in thought about lattes and love. That bottom lip looks like a ripe piece of fruit, waiting to be tasted. I really need to stop devouring this man with my eyes.

The woman behind me pokes me in the back this time. I step up to the counter as I hear her mutter, "Honestly. No shame."

My cheeks heat, but I clear my throat. "A hot chocolate please with double peppermint. And a cinnamon bun."

"Mmm-hmm." The girl behind the counter in her black apron and messy bun takes down my order on the cash register. Her gaze flicks to the man I've been ogling. I'm not the only one who's noticed him. I sneak another glance at him too.

"Peppermint hot chocolate for Kyle," one of the baristas calls out and the man lifts his hand, stepping forward.

Kyle. I like the sound of that. And he ordered peppermint hot chocolate too! That's a sign, right? I'm taking that as a sign.

"It'll be a few minutes," the girl says.

"No worries." I pay and step to the side just as the man, Kyle, walks toward a table. Bad luck there. I'd kind of been hoping we would be waiting for our drinks at the same time and I could oh so casually start up a conversation. I try to think of an excuse to go and talk to him now, but nothing that doesn't say "desperate single woman" comes to mind.

He sits down, takes a sip of the hot chocolate and pulls his phone out of his jacket pocket. He's still frowning and I have the urge to make him smile, or laugh even. The frown is adorable, but it makes me wonder how his smile would look.

"However," a loud voice says, making me jump, "Detective Reece believes that these murders are all the work of one serial killer."

The woman behind me in line is now standing beside me with her phone out, volume way up, watching the news. I inch away from her as I see Kyle look toward us at the noise. I try to smile at him, but he goes back to his own phone.

"No one had previously linked these deaths because there are so many differences," a new male voice says from her phone. I wish she would turn the volume down or put in headphones. "For example, all the deceased live in different locations, have different ethnic backgrounds, and are different ages. They died at different times and in different ways. For example, Benjamin Johnson, age 45, was living in Illinois when he was found dead in his apartment, having died from a gunshot wound during a burglary gone wrong."

I cringe, trying to get rid of the mental image of a man being shot to death. I really hate the news.

"Dominic Rusher, age 52, lived in Washington, D.C. at the time of his passing. The cause of death was determined to be an accidental overdose of his heart medication. And Liam Alvarez, age 48, lived in Mexico where he drowned in his outdoor pool. Police suspected suicide."

I swallow and debate leaving without my hot chocolate.

"I could go on with the differences," the detective continues. "However, each of these five deaths in the past three and a half years have several things in common," he says. "The first being that each of these men were in fact, men.

I focus on Kyle, hoping his good looks will distract me.

"The next, and here is what really caught my attention, is that they were all incredibly wealthy. Each of them was at least a millionaire, with one of the five deceased men - Jacob Giovanni - being a billionaire."

Kyle sighs and leans back in his chair, sipping at his hot chocolate. I watch his Adams apple bob as he swallows.

"None of them were married," the detective continues. "I know I have spoken about these connections before and so far, it has seemed that these coincidences were just that - coincidences. But as I have dug deeper, I was able to uncover something new that has convinced me the deaths are linked."

Setting down his hot chocolate, Kyle glances around the shop, almost as if he is looking for something. His gaze pauses on a couple different people and he seems to study them for a moment before moving on.

"I have discovered that at the time of their death, all five of these men were engaged to be married. And - here is what absolutely convinces me - in each of these cases, the fiancee has been named as the sole inheritor in the man's will."

Kyle's gaze lands squarely on me. I look away, feeling like a middle school girl caught staring at her secret crush. I know my cheeks are giving me away. I was born with the "Hillsdale

Curse" as my mom calls it. Hillsdale girls can never hide their emotions. Our faces might as well be blinking neon signs.

"This information was hard to come by as the fiances are nowhere to be found and the corresponding legal documents are not shared publicly." I seriously wish this detective would shut up. "In each case, the fiance had a different name, and unfortunately we have no descriptions to go off of. But I am convinced that the person responsible for these murders is none other than the fiance herself."

Kyle stands, phone in hand. I watch from the corner of my eye, heart rate picking up, as he walks directly toward me. I step out of his way, thinking he might need to ask the barista for a sugar packet or a straw or something. Instead, he stops right in front of me.

# Chapter Four

"IT SEEMS THIS is a woman who targets rich single men for their money," I hear the lady's phone say as I look up into Kyle's rich brown eyes. And then the sound of the phone seems to fall away.

My breath catches in my chest. His brown eyes are even softer and deeper when I'm looking right into them, and I feel myself melting.

"Hello," he says. His voice is deeper than I expected.

"Hey!" My voice comes out a squeak and I clear my throat. Sound casual! "Hey."

"I know this may seem unusual," he says, "but I have a request."

"All right," I say, wondering what on earth this man could need from the likes of little old Amy-Kate.

He gestures at his phone. "My granny is trying to arrange a date for me with a woman she met on a flight back from Australia."

Did he just call his grandmother "granny"? That was adorable. Also, his "granny" was just in Australia! How awesome is that?

"She fears for my love life, which is ever so kind of her. But the last three dates she arranged all ended in disaster. And these were not small disasters. I'll spare you the details, but there were ambulances and fire trucks involved."

I try not to laugh. "So, basically you fear for your life?"

He lets out a breath. "Exactly. She's a sweet woman and incredibly dear to me. I have no desire to hurt her feelings, and so I have determined the only way to kindly turn down her match-making offer is to prove to her that I can find a Valentine's date for myself."

My heart skips a beat. "A Valentine's date?" Is he seriously asking me on a date? On Valentine's Day? This is way too good to be true.

"It's unusual, I know," he says. "We've just met and I'm a perfect stranger to you. But if you could help me out, I'd be ever so obliged."

I blink at him. "Help you out," I say slowly, "by going on a date with you?"

"I know it's a lot to ask! If you already have plans-"

"No! Uh. I mean, no. I don't have plans. No plans at all!

I mean-" Could I sound more desperate? "If I did have plans I'm sure I could cancel them. To help you out. As a favor."

He lets out a breath, relieved. Did he honestly think I'd turn him down? "Are you sure?" he asks. "I don't want to inconvenience you."

"Oh, I'm sure. I'm very sure." I need to stop talking. He's going to realize I am way too eager and change his mind.

"That would be so splendid! Thank you so much!"

Splendid? I like the way he talks.

"Would you be amenable to going to the King's Valley restaurant?" he asks.

"King's Valley?" Good heavens! Is he serious? He has to be joking. That place is crazy expensive. And for a first date?

"Do you not like their food?"

How would I know if I liked their food? I give a small laugh and shrug like being asked out to the most expensive restaurant in town by the most handsome man I've ever met is an everyday occurrence. "Uh, sure. King's Valley is fine with me. If it's fine with you!"

His face relaxes. "Excellent. Should we meet there at six? I would offer to pick you up, but I know you might be wary of a man you've only just met."

"Yeah. Good point. I guess I don't know if you're a serial killer or not." I wince and glance at the woman with her phone. She's scowling at me. I quickly look away.

He chuckles. "Exactly. Though, I promise I'm not."

"Well, that makes me feel lots better." I smile to show I'm teasing. Am I flirting with him? "We can meet there."

"Would it be alright if I asked for your number?"

"Oh, of course!" My cheeks turn darker pink. This is really happening!

He hands his phone to me, already pulled up to a new contact screen. It's warm and I try not to think about how warm his hands must be as I put in my first name and number, my hands shaking ever so slightly.

"Amy-Kate," he reads off the phone when I hand it back to him. "Well, Amy-Kate, it was a pleasure to meet you. I'm Kyle." He holds out his hand, all formal, and we shake.

"Good to meet you, Kyle."

He gives me a small smile and my heart leaps. His smile is even more adorable than his frown, with laugh lines like parenthesis drawing attention to that full lower lip. I'm blushing like crazy, so I just raise my hand and turn away. And walk right into a table.

I stifle my "ow," walk around the table, and glance back to see if he saw. He totally did. I raise my hand again. "I'm good!"

He nods, smiles a little again, and goes to retrieve his hot chocolate from the table.

I'm going on a date! With an amazingly attractive man! On Valentine's Day! The love gods have finally seen fit to bless me!

"Oh, one more thing," he says, turning back to me. "I

should make my expectations clear so there isn't any confusion. While I am grateful to you, I am really not ready for any sort of commitment. So, if it's alright with you, just think of this as a meeting between friends."

"Oh." So much for blessings from the love gods. "Right. Of course." I make a face. "Commitment. Who needs it?"

He nods. "Excellent. Six o'clock then." He gives another small closed-lip smile and pushes out the door.

I sag into the nearest chair and let out my breath in a big huff, blowing my bangs to the side.

"Girl," says the barista, walking up to my table and handing over my peppermint hot chocolate and cinnamon bun. "I don't care what that man says about it not being a real date. You're never going to find a better-looking man than that. Take what you can get, I say."

I laugh and see the woman with her phone scowl deeper at us.

Any date is better than no date, right?

# Chapter Five

MOM SAYS I'M too desperate, but when all your friends are dating or have even gotten married and are posting sappy pictures of happy couples on social media, you start to go a little insane.

Standing on the sidewalk, I look up at the sign over the restaurant door. "King's Valley Restaurant" is written in red cursive on a gold background. I've seen this place before, but I never imagined I would be walking inside it, for a date! It's an imposing building with white columns and scroll work which I am sure some architecture guru could give me a name for. I feel awkward just standing on the street. Should I wait inside?

I've been a scatter-brained mess all day, off in Lala Land with Mr. Kyle Dreamy, and my boss wasn't too happy. She yelled at me, which would usually ruin my day, but nothing could pop this glowing bubble around me. Nothing, that is, except for my silent phone.

I look both ways, up and down the street, and then at the time again, lighting up my phone screen: 6:04. He's going to call any second. Or text. Or just show up. I'm sure of it. I bite my lip.

6:05.

There's nothing to distract myself with. I look over my outfit again. At home, I'd felt that maybe it was a bit over the top, but now, watching men in suits and women in basically prom dresses entering the restaurant, I feel under dressed. I was going for cute and dressy - a white skirt that swishes when I turn, a loose pink top and my pink heels. I'd thought the heels might be a bit much. But I wanted something about my outfit to say that this was a date and not just a casual hangout. I tousle my loose hair. It was brown and a little longer than my shoulders. Now I wonder why I bothered with earrings when my hair effectively covers them.

I apply more lip gloss and check my phone again.

6:08.

Maybe he's waiting inside? Maybe he thinks I'm late and doesn't want to call while I might be driving?

I straighten my shoulders and face the doorway. I'm going to have to venture inside. Alone.

Swallowing, I push open one of the double doors painted red with gold trim. And my breath catches.

The entry to the restaurant is incredible. The floor is tiled in gold and white. Gold columns travel up to a vaulted ceiling painted in white fluffy clouds where a chandelier sparkles like the sun. This is a restaurant? It looks like a palace!

"Welcome to King's Valley!"

I start and turn to the two girls behind a desk. They have their hair in buns and wear identical black dresses and gold earrings.

"How many are in your party?" one of them asks.

"Uh, two?"

"Right this way!"

"Actually, I was wondering if he's already here and waiting for me? Did a guy come in alone? His name is Kyle."

The two girls glance at each other. "I don't think so," one of them says.

"Oh. Okay. I'll just wait for him then. Before being seated."

"Okay!"

I smile tightly and step to the side of the room. There are benches with soft cushions, but I don't sit. He'll be here any second.

I shift my weight and try not to stare at the decorations. Potted plants that I know are real. I can smell them. I'm tempted to ask where the restroom is just so I can ogle at it. I imagine it might actually smell nice.

I check my phone again. 6:09. I blow out my breath.

Maybe it's a joke. Maybe he was filming me in that coffee shop for a reality tv show. Maybe he just collects random girl's numbers because he's a creeper. Or just because he could.

A happy couple enters the restaurant hand in hand, the girl giggling. I give them a tight smile, but they don't notice me. One of the girls behind the counter leads them back.

I wait. The hostess comes back from showing the couple to their table. 6:15.

The hostesses look at me and give me a smile when I look back. It looks like a sad smile. They pity me. I pity me!

I stare up at the ceiling with its blue sky and fluffy clouds. I'm not going to cry.

He had seemed so sincere.

My phone buzzes and I start, grabbing it out of my pocket so fast I fumble it and drop it on the floor with a clatter. I wince and hurry to pick it up, face burning. It's just my mom.

Mom: Happy Valentines Day, sweetie! Just remember, you don't need a man to complete you. -Mom

I stuff the phone back in my pocket. Nice timing, Mom.

The hostesses are watching me. Kyle isn't here. I might as well wait outside where these girls can't keep looking at me sadly. Poor girl. No date on Valentine's Day!

"I'll be back," I say to them and push back through the door and into the cold. This is so stupid. I should have dressed warmer. Forget being cute.

My phone buzzes again. I react more slowly this time,

sure it's mom sending another message.

Fred: Hey, are we still on for tonight? I came by your place, but no one was home.

My heart plummets. Fred! I totally forgot that I told him we could hang out tonight! Poor guy!

Me: Oh my goodness! I am so sorry! Something came up last minute and I forgot to text you! Worst friend ever!

Fred: No worries. Is everything okay?

Me: Yeah. I'm fine. Just need to cancel for tonight. Is that okay?

Fred: Okay. Rain check?

Me: Of course!

Fred: See you later. Have a good evening!

I stick the phone back in my pocket and rub my temples. I feel so bad! Fred will understand, right? I mean, I know we'll still be friends. Our friendship has been tested more severely than a canceled hang out, but still. I feel bad.

And where is Kyle? I just canceled on my best friend for him and he doesn't even have the decency to show up?

I think of Kyle's hesitant smile and warm eyes. He had seemed relieved when I agreed to go on a date with him. So concerned that I would think he was crazy. Just thinking about his dreamy looks - that wavy hair, just long enough to kiss the tops of his eyebrows, and those brown eyes with long lashes any girl would envy - makes my heart flutter. I really thought that he would come.

But he never gave me his number. Maybe that should have been a clue.

I keep waiting though, hoping against hope that he'll come dashing up the street, all out of breath, and say how sorry he is for being late. That his car broke down and he had to run here on foot, but he wouldn't miss this date for the world.

Yeah right.

At 6:30 I stuff my hands into my armpits for warmth and trudge back to my car. If he does make it to the restaurant eventually, he can call me. I'm not standing in this cold and humiliation any longer.

I drive home in silence, blinking fast to keep my vision clear. That shiny golden bubble around me fizzles away letting in the cold dreary reality. I've been duped. Stood-up. He just wanted to mess with me. It was some stupid Valentine's Day joke. Maybe he'd noticed me mooning over him and decided to have some fun at my expense.

I park the car and get out, ready to get out of these heels and into something comfortable. Ready to curl up under my covers with some ice cream and tissues.

I trudge up the stairs to my apartment, feeling more exhausted than I should, like the disappointment has stolen my energy. As I reach the third floor, something on my welcome mat catches my attention. A red heart-shaped box.

My pulse leaps for a second. But it can't be from Kyle. He doesn't know where I live.

I pick it up and see the sticky note on the front.

Hey Amy-Kate, I hope your day is fantastic! -Fred

My throat closes up a bit. That was so nice of him.

I shouldn't have canceled. If I'd just hung out with my best friend instead of waiting around for someone too good to be true, I could have had a fun evening. I really am a terrible friend. At least I'll have chocolate to eat tonight as I wallow in my misery.

I push into my apartment and let the tears come.

# Chapter Six

"YOU SHOULDN'T BE giving your number out to strange men," Mom says, unlocking the door to the flower shop and stepping inside.

"That's not the point, Mom!" The door shuts behind us with a tinkle of bells and I inhale the heady aroma of lilacs, peonies, and green things. Mom always tries to talk me into working at the shop with her, and honestly it's tempting. I love the flowers, and I have a knack for arranging them. But having my mom as my boss? No thank you. So instead, I'm wasting my life away in a cubicle mushed between nineteen other cubicles, with one dead potted plant in the corner that apparently no one can be bothered to remove. Sometimes I wonder about my life choices.

"The point," I say, following her to the counter as she

flicks on lights, "is that some jerk stood me up!"

"Yes, well, that's what you get for being so loose!"

"This isn't the 1900's. It's perfectly normal to give your number to a nice handsome man when he asks you out."

"Nice? I thought you just said he was a jerk."

I sigh. "Point taken. I guess I should just give up, accept my life as a single woman and go adopt some cats."

"You're so dramatic." Mom dusts off the countertop with her hand and boots up the ancient computer to the side. "When I was your age I wasn't worried about what men were thinking about me. I was content with my life."

"When you were my age," I say, "you were already dating Dad!"

"Yes, but I didn't need him to complete me. I had my own life. My own passions and interests. He was the desperate one out of the two of us, honestly."

I hop up on the counter and put my chin in my palm. "I just wanted you to say something like, 'That sounds terrible! How could someone do that to my sweet daughter!'"

"That sounds terrible," Mom repeats in a monotone, squinting at the computer. "How could someone do that to my sweet daughter."

I roll my eyes. "Thanks, Mom. I feel so much better." My phone buzzes and I straighten my leg to wriggle it free from my jeans pocket. Why are the pockets in women's jeans so tiny?

Rachelle: Rude! How could he?? And on Valentine's Day! If you need to vent, call me!

"See?" I say, holding up the phone. "Rachelle knows the correct response when I tell her I got stood up by a jerk!"

Mom realizes where I'm sitting and shoos me down. "Make yourself useful. If you feel so bad, why don't you distract yourself by making some nice arrangements. That always clears your head."

"It's the day after Valentine's Day," I say. "Everyone already bought all their flowers." But I wander over to the large refrigerator anyway, looking through the glass doors at the bouquets and arrangements displayed. There are a couple left over Valentine's Day ones, but if I take out the glittery pink and red hearts on sticks and add in some other color, yellow maybe, I can turn them into something fresh and not so lovey-dovey. It's Saturday, so I have the whole day to work, just me and the flowers.

I take a moment to text Rachelle back.

Me: I'll call you in a bit. I'm helping Mom at the flower shop.

I'm just sliding open one of the doors when Mom says, "Actually, Amy-Kate, there is something I've been wanting to talk to you about."

I pause. "Yeah?" She sounds so serious I wonder if I'm in trouble.

But she smiles at me across the counter. "I've been thinking of retiring, you know."

"Wait, really? You're not that old!"

She shrugs. "I'm getting up there in age. But I was thinking, when I retire, I'd like to pass this flower shop along to you."

"Wait, what?" Maybe I should have seen this coming, me being her daughter and all, but honestly the thought had never crossed my mind. "Me?" My heart expands at the thought and I look around at the flowers and the old computer and the rack of greeting cards.

"I think you would be perfect for it," says Mom. "After all, you were practically raised here. You know all the ins and outs and you have a natural talent for arranging."

"I-" I swallow as I see the white board behind Mom where orders are written up with dates and flowers and prices and locations. My heart sinks. "I don't think I could do it."

Mom frowns. "Why not?"

"It's so much! I can arrange some flowers, sure, but I've never been good at the scheduling and financing and things like that. You know that!"

Mom rolls her eyes. "You are perfectly capable. And if you're so worried about it, hire someone to help with it. We've been thinking of hiring someone anyway."

I shake my head. "I really don't think I could do it. I mean, I barely make it to my day job on time every day! How could I manage a whole business by myself?"

"Well, you don't have to decide right now. But think about it, okay?"

I swallow. Thinking about it isn't going to change the fact that I'm not competent enough to run my own business. Moms always think their children are more capable than they actually are. And helping arrange some bouquets on weekends is very different from managing the entire company. I would hate to take over and have it all fall apart. Mom would be devastated. I would be devastated. Mom built this company herself. I'm not going to be the one to make it fall apart. But all I say is, "Yeah, sure."

The bell jingles. I look up to see Fred entering the shop. He almost has to duck to get through the door without hitting his head. I swear he gets taller every day.

"Hey!" I say.

"Why hello, Mr. Thompson," says Mom, giving him a huge smile. "So good to see you!" Mom is stubbornly team Fred, even though I've told her we're just friends and there is absolutely no chemistry between us. I think she's just hoping for tall grandchildren. We're all terribly short in the Hillsdale family.

"Hello, Mrs. Hillsdale," says Fred, and his smile, as always, is big and bright. "How are you two doing today?"

"The sun is shining, the flowers are blooming," says Mom. "What more could I ask for?"

Fred nods and turns to me. "How about you, Amy-Kate?

How did things go yesterday?"

"Ugh." I make a face. "Not so great. Sorry for canceling on you last minute."

Fred shrugs and leans against the refrigerator as I squat and start rummaging through the arrangements, deciding what I want to work on first.

"No worries," he says.

"It was just that there was this guy who asked me out last minute."

Fred raises his eyebrows. "Yeah?"

"Yeah. But I shouldn't have wasted my time. He totally stood me up!"

Something crosses Fred's face, almost like relief. But then he makes a face. "That's so lame! Who would do that?"

"I know right? See, Mom. This is the kind of response I was looking for!"

She chuckles. "Good thing Fred stopped by then."

I heft one of the arrangements from the refrigerator and stand. Fred jumps forward to take it from me.

"Where do you want it?" he asks.

"Just on the counter there. Thanks." I follow him over. "Anyway, pretty sure I was part of some reality TV show or something where he sees how many girl's numbers he can get in one day." I push up my sleeves and consider the arrangement. It's got pink and red tulips and glittery foam hearts on sticks. I start pulling out the hearts. "Or maybe something bad happened to him and he's in the hospital dying and I'm a terrible person for being mad at him."

Fred crosses his arms and leans against the counter. "Maybe. But not likely."

"Anyway, Valentine's Day was miserable, as usual. I'm glad it's over!" I toss the foam hearts in the trash. "Thank you for the chocolates though! They were delicious! I should have just hung out with you. Sorry again for canceling."

Fred smiles. "Of course! We should get together some time."

"Sure." I look over at Mom who has stopped clicking around on the computer and is beaming at the two of us. I turn pink and look away, sure she is thinking that hanging out means we're going to elope. Why does she have to be so obvious about it? And seriously, why Fred? He's nice enough, but he's not exactly what I'd call amazingly handsome. He's kind of geeky looking. And just nerdy in general.

"I'm going to grab some more flowers," Mom says and I swear she winks as she goes to the employees only door. Good grief.

The bell jingles over the front door again and I turn, then gasp, grabbing Fred by the arm and pulling him down with me as I duck behind the counter. I don't know why I grabbed him. It just seemed like the thing to do.

The man who just entered the flower shop is Kyle.

# Chapter Seven

"WHAT IN THE-" Mom says, looking at me hiding in my hiding spot.

"Shhhh!" I peek around the side of the counter.

Dang, I'd forgotten exactly how good-looking Kyle is. He's wearing the same outfit - blue suit coat with a white shirt, no tie. He's looking around uncertainly, lips pressed together, brows a little pinched, and the look is adorable on him. His brown hair is curling over his forehead just so and I can imagine exactly how soft it would be if I ran my fingers through it. I shake myself mentally. This is not the time to get swoony over him. Not again.

"Is that the guy?" Fred whispers, peeking around the counter over my head.

I nod.

"Looks like he's not in the hospital," says Fred.

"Welcome," says Mom, nudging us out of the way with her foot as she steps out from behind the counter to greet him. "What can I help you with?"

"Good morning," he says, stepping forward to meet her, hand out to shake hers.

I shrink back out of sight.

"I'd like a bouquet to give to someone as an apology," he says.

Fred's eyebrows shoot up and he gives me a look.

An apology? He's sorry? About standing me up? Is he seriously buying me flowers? The only flowers I've ever gotten were from an awkward guy in high school when he asked me to prom. I found out afterwords I was his third choice. He used the same bouquet to ask out all three of us, one after the other. I was the only one desperate enough to say yes.

"Of course! We have lots of options." Mom leads Kyle over to the glass doored fridge to look at the arrangements I haven't had the chance to re-do yet. I peek around the corner of the counter to watch.

Kyle considers the arrangements. "These all look excellent. Do you have a recommendation?"

The bell over the door tinkles again. Seriously? And I thought the day after Valentine's Day was going to be dead. Fred and I both stick our heads out further to see who it is now.

"There you are!" a woman gushes, clicking into the store in red heels, bosom first. "I've been looking everywhere for you!" She has a tiny little waist that is at odds with her voluptuous blond hair, fat red lips, and too much makeup.

I watch, feeling a weight settle in the pit of my stomach, as she hurries to Kyle, taking little mincing steps in those ridiculous heels. She clutches his arm in both of hers, and then, with that same concerned expression pinching Kyle's brows, she plants a smacking kiss on his cheek. It leaves a lipstick smear that she wipes off with her thumb, one long red nail almost gouging his cheek.

"Oh, darling," she coos. "Are you buying flowers for me? How sweet of you! But you know you don't have to." She leans forward, more than is necessary, to look into the case, showing off what can only be surgically created cleavage.

I wince and look away. Fred is already looking at the floor, face pink. Poor guy.

"Oh! Look at these!" the woman gushes. "They're just darling!"

I peek at Kyle again. He's giving my mom an apologetic smile like he understands how painful proximity to this woman can be.

The woman tugs on his arm, drawing his attention. She points one long red nail. "That one. It's perfect!"

Mom glances at Kyle but he doesn't notice. So Mom slides open the refrigerator door and hefts out the arrangement. I'm surprised to see it's one of my creations. I would have expected this woman to choose something garish and over the top - one of the left-over Valentine bouquets with too many sparkly red and pink hearts. But I grudgingly admitted she has good taste. In both flowers and men.

I glance back at Kyle and see him frowning. Directly at me. "Amy-Kate?"

I jump to my feet, hitting my head on the counter ledge, and let out a cry.

Mom and the woman turn to look at me too. Fred gets to his feet beside me.

"Were you down there this whole time?" asks Kyle as I massage my head, wincing.

"Still can't find that lost earring," I say to Mom. "That's too bad! Thanks for helping to look, Fred!"

Mom raises her eyebrows, but doesn't comment. She's always more wily than I give her credit for. Or maybe she just knows it's a lame excuse and doesn't want to get dragged into this lie with me.

"Yep. Well. Better go and... do stuff." I grab Fred's arm, and drag him through the employees-only door, letting it close behind us. Then I turn and peek through the round window in the door.

Kyle's looking right at me, eyebrows drawn together like he is deeply concerned for my mental well-being. I duck, feeling like an idiot in more ways than one. I am sure my face is scarlet.

"Stupid. Stupid!" I mutter. "Of course he has a girlfriend! I should have known someone that handsome asking me out was too good to be true! And of course the flowers weren't for me!"

Fred is frowning at me.

"What?"

"Want me to go give him a piece of my mind about treating you like that?"

"What? You mean like punch him?" The idea of Fred trying to punch someone is hilarious. But then I take in his broad shoulders. In my head, he's still that scrawny kid from high school, but he might actually be able to take on Kyle now. The thought of him wanting to for my sake is kind of touching. "That's all right."

I press my ear to the door to hear what's happening on the other side. It's childish, but more childish than asking out a stranger when you already have a girlfriend? I think not.

"I'm just an idiot for thinking he was interested in me!" I say.

"You're not an idiot," says Fred. "He's an idiot for standing you up."

"I bet he had some fight with this girl," I say, "and asked me out as a way to get back at her during their fight. But now they've made up so he doesn't need me anymore."

"You were going to write something sweet on the card,

weren't you?" the woman is saying, her tone all sappy. "Were these to say you're sorry? Because you know I forgive you! Just because I haven't made the vow yet doesn't mean I'm going to change my mind about you. I will love you until the day you die. That's what fiances do!"

My stomach clenches. Fiance? I risk another peek through the window and sure enough, there is the gigantic rock glittering on her finger. How did I not notice that? Kyle, who is taking his credit card back from Mom, turns his head towards me again and I duck.

Why do I care so much anyway? It's not like I actually know this guy. He's a stranger. An unfairly handsome stranger who decided to have a laugh on my behalf. I frown and hear the bells tinkle as they leave the shop. He's a jerk. That's all there is to it. I've dealt with plenty of jerks before. And he is no different. Well, maybe a little more good looking than the average jerk, but it's what's on the inside that counts, right?

The staff door I'm standing in front of bangs into me. "Ow!" I jump away. How many times am I going to get injured today? Isn't my wounded heart enough?

Mom stands in the doorway, arms crossed. "I'm going to hazard a guess that he was the coffee shop man?" Mom asks. "Either that or you have suddenly developed a phobia of attractive men."

"You thought he was attractive too?" For some reason the fact that my mom found a man besides my late father attractive is weirdly disconcerting, though now that I stop to think about it for half a second, of course she does. Probably every woman in the universe thinks Kyle is attractive.

Mom rolls her eyes. "I'll take that as a yes. Do you want me to bring down the wrath of my knitting group on him? Old ladies with pointy sticks can be very threatening."

"That's what I asked," says Fred. "Well, not the knitting part."

I laugh. "No. I don't think so, as much as I appreciate the offer."

"Well, you let me know. As much as I don't like you mooning over boys all the time, it makes my blood boil to think that an engaged man was toying with you."

I feel oddly touched by this statement. Mom usually doesn't sympathize much when I break up with boyfriends or am crossed in love and have my tender heart broken. It gets broken a lot, honestly. Maybe that's why. But this show of indignation on my behalf is rather sweet and motherly.

All I say is, "I do not moon over boys!"

"He's engaged?" says Fred, outraged.

Mom holds up her hands. "Enough of this boy talk! What we need is some good hard work to take our minds off of everything."

That's more like her. Hard work is the cure-all as far as she's concerned. I would have preferred a chick-flick and some ice cream, but I'll call Rachelle about that later.

"You want to help out?" I ask Fred, who still seems to be seething on my behalf.

He nods, all serious. "Let's do this!"

# Chapter Eight

I THROW MYSELF into flower arranging with a passion. It isn't something people typically think of when they want to release anger, like weed whacking or hitting a baseball where you can get aggressive without actually hurting anything. This is a different sort of relief. When I'm with the flowers, I move all other thoughts aside, letting my mind breathe. It's like stepping into a pocket of fresh air.

I re-do all the old Valentine's Day bouquets, making them look like spring. Then I get started on the order mom has for an upcoming wedding. Mom hires people to work on these things during the week, but I like to help out when I can. Especially the weekends. The bride's chosen yellow and pink as her colors and is letting us be in charge of the types of flowers for the bouquet. She gave us a few pictures of what she likes, but it's mostly up to us. I like it when I can get creative with wedding bouquets.

I hum to myself as I try out different flowers here and some foliage there. And I absolutely do not think about Kyle. At all. Not even for a second.

Mom finally interrupts my creating to say, "I'm heading out. Do you want to finish working on that tomorrow? We don't need it until Monday."

I glance out the windows. It's dark outside. I hadn't realized how late it was. Fred left hours ago.

"I'm almost done. I might as well finish tonight."

"All right. Be sure the lights are all off and the door is locked behind you when you leave."

I nod and pull a yellow craspedia flower out from deep inside the bouquet, making its bright yellow bulb stand out. "Okay."

Mom leaves and I go back to humming and arranging. It's so soothing. Flowers don't judge. Flowers are unique but easy to please. If you treat them right, they'll do what you want. There's nothing frustrating about flowers or foliage.

When I finish the bouquet, it's heavy in my hands. I tie a pink ribbon around it and leave the tails trailing. It looks breath-taking. One of my better creations. I hope the bride likes it.

I place it in a heavy-duty vase, slide it into the refrigerator, and turn out the lights. As I step outside, the sharp cold air invades my lungs after the sweet warmth of the flower shop. I cough.

"Amy-Kate?"

I jump.

"Sorry to startle you!" Kyle stands up from a sidewalk bench.

I immediately blush and look away from him, refusing to be taken in by his insanely good looks a second time. "What are you doing here?" I fish around in my purse for my phone just in case I need to call 911 about this guy stalking me. "You freaked me out, stepping out of the shadows like that! What are you, some creeper?"

"Goodness, no! I apologize. I was hoping for the chance to speak with you."

"So you creepily waited outside, looking in the window at me, instead of just texting like a normal person?"

"Unfortunately, my phone no longer works," he says. "I had to purchase a new one, but was unable to transfer over the contacts. That's why I never called."

I scoff and turn to lock the flower shop doors. "Uh huh. So, it had nothing to do with your fiance? Good to know that you don't mind cheating on her."

"That woman is not my fiance!" He says this so vehemently that I turn to look at him. Big mistake. He's looking at me so imploringly it makes my heart trip. His hair is mussed like he's been running his fingers through it and it makes me want to run my own fingers through it.

I look away. "What? So, she's crazy? She bought herself that ring?" I watch him out of the corner of my eyes. I can't help it.

He adjusts his suit jacket, hands on his lapels, like he's nervous. "No. I bought her the ring and proposed a couple months ago. We used to be engaged. But then I broke it off."

I roll my eyes. "I think you forgot to tell her that." I start walking away. Then I pause, remembering the news report in the coffee shop. "Wait, she was your fiance?" I don't wait for an answer. "And she's desperate to get back together? Did she ask to be written into your will by any chance?"

The line between his eyebrows deepens. "As my fiance, yes. Why do you ask?"

I tap my chin thoughtfully. I have no idea what Kyle is worth, financially, but he seems loaded. "Have you seen the news lately?"

"The news?" He is clearly not on the same wavelength as me.

"There's some story about a crazy serial killer fiance who gets written into rich men's wills and then takes them out and runs off with all their money."

He lets out a surprised breath. "Jillian might be intent on winning me back, but she's hardly the serial killer type."

I shrug and start walking again. "You never know. I'd watch out for her if I was you."

Kyle strides over, easily keeping pace beside me.

"I just want to apologize," he says. "I would have stopped by earlier, once I realized you worked here, but I decided to come when you closed so I didn't make you feel uncomfortable in front of your boss."

I blink. "My boss? Oh, you mean my mom? Yeah, she would have chased you out of the store with a thorn branch, and then sent her knitting club to hunt you down."

His brow furrows.

"Never mind." I turn away and start walking. "Apology not accepted. Now, please let me walk home in peace."

He jogs up beside me. "I am sincerely sorry. I don't like the thought that I have hurt you in any way. The bouquet was meant for you. To apologize."

"How were you going to get it to me?" I ask. "You don't even have my number!"

"I was thinking I'd drop it off at that coffee shop where we met. I figured you might go back there, and so I'd give it to the barista and ask her to deliver it when you showed up."

I blink. That's actually a pretty good idea. And really sweet of him.

"It wasn't going to be a real date anyway," I say. "Why are you so worked up about this?"

"Honestly," he says. "I'm not certain."

"Well, that's too bad for you." I speed up the pace a little. "Now, if you'll excuse me-"

He rushes to stand in front of me, blocking my path. "I want to ask you out again."

I laugh out loud. "Seriously?" I avoid his warm brown eyes. I am not getting sucked into this. Not again.

"I'm serious!" he says. "I want to make it up to you, for not showing last time."

"Look," I say, holding up my hands and stepping around him. "You've obviously got your own girl problems and I don't really want to be mixed up in them, so please. Just leave."

He gives me a forlorn expression, like a little puppy dog I just told off for peeing on the carpet. Hands in pockets and head down he looks defeated. "Amy-Kate," he says quietly. "There is something different about you." His cheeks turn slightly pink as he looks up at me through those long lashes.

He looks adorable, too adorable to be real, like an Anime character all the girls fall for. My heart catches in my chest. But this is ridiculous, and I am not going to agree to a date with this guy only to get stood up again.

"I noticed it at the coffee shop," he says. "And I haven't been able to put you out of my mind since then."

My heart is definitely picking up the pace. Traitor.

"Look, apology accepted," I say. "Does that help?"

"A little," he admits.

"Good." I start walking, but again, he catches up and starts walking beside me.

"If you're still hesitant because of Jillian - the woman you saw at your flower shop - I promise you that we are no longer together. She was devastated when I broke things off with her and has been trying to get back together with me ever since. She's in denial, trying to pretend that we never really broke up. Honestly, the longer I was with her the more unstable she seemed. That was the reason for ending things in the first place. I don't like to fight with her about it in public, but it's getting out of hand. I apologize for the scene she caused."

"It sounds like she needs some serious help. Or... she's that serial killer." I'm liking this theory more and more.

Kyle ignores this last comment. "I've been trying to convince her to see a therapist or counselor, but she refuses. I don't know how to get her to realize I am not getting back together with her. Ever again."

"Wait, wait, wait. I see what going on." I stop walking and face him, hands on hips. "That's the real reason you want me to go out with you, isn't it? You want her to see that you've moved on. It has nothing to do with me, or your sweet granny setting you up on bad dates. This is all about your crazy ex!"

"No! Goodness no."

I shake my head.

"I was telling the truth about my granny," he says. "She has been trying to find someone for me ever since I broke up with Jillian. And honestly, you intrigue me, Amy-Kate." He looks up at me, almost shyly. "I've never met anyone quite like you. Please, just give me a chance."

I contemplate him.

He seems so hopeful.

"Give me your number," I say. "Your new phone number."

"What?" He blinks.

"Give me your number. I'll put it in my phone, and then you can wait at home and wonder if I'm ever going to call you. Sound good?" I give him a sweet smile.

"Are you being serious?"

"Deadly serious."

"I will be glad to give you my number." He gives me the digits, and I type them into my phone, putting his name as Kyle the Jerk. It's childish. I know. But I have to remind my future self not to call this guy. No matter how charming he is.

"Well, you might hear from me sometime," I say, turning away. "Or, you might not. Guess you'll have to wait and find out!" I wave without turning back towards him. And at last, he doesn't follow me.

# Chapter Nine

I SIT ON MY BED and stare at Kyle's name in my phone. I haven't contacted him. At least not yet. What am I thinking?

I wonder if he's sitting somewhere staring at his phone, wondering if I'll call. Probably not.

He stood me up. But he didn't mean to. His phone was broken. If he's telling the truth.

He's engaged. Except he isn't anymore. He just has a crazy ex. If he's telling the truth.

I can understand crazy exes. I've had a few of those myself. Well, okay. Maybe not pretend-we're-still-together crazy. His lady takes desperate to a whole new level.

Is he telling the truth? I decide to give him the benefit of the doubt.

I click the call button.

He answers before the second ring. Maybe he was waiting for my call after all.

"Hello?" he says, uncertainly.

"Hey, Kyle."

"Amy-Kate?"

I fight down a blush. Good grief. One word into our conversation and I'm already blushing.

"I said I'd call," I say. "And so I want to keep my word. Because that's something that's important to me. In case you were wondering."

There's a beat of silence. "I am so sorry, Amy-Kate."

Maybe I'm being a little harsh.

"Will you allow me take you on a date?" he asks. "I promise nothing will get in the way of it this time." He sounds so hopeful, and yet so uncertain, like he's afraid I'm going to crush his hopes and dreams.

I let him hang, just for a moment. I can't help it. "I guess so," I say. "But it had better be a good one."

I can hear the smile in his voice as he said, "I promise this will be the most wonderful date of your life!"

I struggle to keep my own mouth straight. "Good. Five o'clock tonight. Text me the address of where we're going, and I'll meet you there." Just because I'm giving him a chance doesn't mean I trust him yet. So I take my mom's advice and avoid giving out my address to this stranger.

"Deal," he says. "See you then."

I hang up. My smile spreads despite my best efforts to keep it down. I'm going on a date! A real date! I haven't been on one of those in what feels like ages! Not since I broke it off with Gil the dog whisperer. (Don't ask.)

And it's a date with Kyle! The most attractive man I've seen maybe ever. My heart is fluttering like a butterfly. I hug my phone to my chest and let the smile come. If I'm going to give him a chance, then I'm going to give him a real chance. See what he's like.

I laugh.

I'm going on a date!

# Chapter Ten

I STAND OUTSIDE looking at the address in my phone and then back up at the building in front of me.

"Modern Art Museum" the sign reads. The building is red brick and square, sitting on the edge of a large public park with a fountain that isn't turned on yet. I haven't spent much time downtown. The traffic unnerves me. And with both my job and Mom's flower shop being close to my apartment, I don't really have a reason to come down here much. The park looks nice. Maybe we're going to have a picnic in the park. In the cold.

Okay, maybe not.

But a modern art museum? Really?

I look around for Kyle, then decide to go on in without him. If he doesn't show again, I'm going to take Mom's advice about unleashing the knitting club. And maybe see if I can borrow the neighbor's Doberman to sic on him.

Opening the door lets out a wave of warmth, which is welcome after the chilly February weather. I unwrap my scarf as I look around. It's a chic old building with whitewashed brick walls and an enormous sculpture of warped metal taking up the center of the entryway.

There's a desk to the right and the girl behind the desk in hipster glasses is intently staring at her phone and biting her bottom lip.

"Hey," I say, and she jumps and clutches her heart.

"Oh, goodness! You startled me!" She sets her phone down and pushes up her glasses. "I was just watching the news. Have you been following that case with the dead rich guys?"

Not this again. I shake my head. "I don't really watch the news. Too depressing, you know?"

"Yeah, and creepy," she says. "But in a fascinating way! Like reading a murder mystery! Or watching a horror movie."

Both things I don't do. I'm not really into freaking myself out.

"This case is just so intriguing! Did you know the most recent guy was found drowned in his pool? Like, his body was floating there all bloated-"

"Okay," I interrupt. "That is incredibly disturbing."

She grins. "I know."

I think this girl might need some mental help. Maybe

she's the serial killer!

"Are you here for the wine tasting?" she asks, like we weren't just discussing murder.

"Uh."

Someone touches my shoulder and I jump.

"Kyle!"

He's dressed in his classic outfit - blue suit coat and white shirt. I wonder how many of them he owns. He doesn't seem like the type of guy to wear the same clothes multiple days in a row.

"Hello, Amy-Kate," he says. "I apologize for startling you."

My cheeks color. It seems I jump every time I see this man.

"I guess I have the right place," I say, motioning to the girl at the desk. "She said something about a wine tasting?" And something about a serial killer, but it's probably best to try and forget that part.

He smiles. "Yes! I told you this would be the best date of your life! They have wines here tonight that have been imported from all across the globe."

"Wait, really?" I look back at the girl and she nods eagerly.

"Also, there will be cheese from around the world as well," she says. "Both of them are super aged!"

"Super aged, huh?"

She nods again, beaming. "So the two of you will be doing the tour?"

“Absolutely,” says Kyle, striding up to the desk and pulling out his wallet.

The girl quotes the price to him and my jaw falls. He’s paying how much for our first date? But I guess I shouldn’t be surprised. He was going to take me to the King’s Valley Restaurant after all.

Kyle turns back to me and I snap my mouth shut.

“Shall we?” he gestures across the entryway.

“Uh, sure,” I say.

“You can hang your coats here,” the girl says, gesturing to the wall behind the desk where a wooden board with hooks on it is affixed to the wall. “I’ll make sure no one steals them!”

I’m a little more worried about her stealing them than the average person, but Kyle is already taking the back of my coat to help me out of it.

I shrug out of it and his fingers brush the back of my neck sending a delicious shiver down my spine. Kyle hands over my coat and then proceeds to take off his suit coat. For some reason, this makes me blush, like I’m seeing him under-dressed, which is ridiculous. He’s still in a long-sleeve shirt and dress pants, but then he starts to roll up his sleeves, exposing tanned and muscled forearms and I feel like my face might melt off.

Good grief. So he has nice arms. Really nice arms, with perfect arm hairs that make me want to touch him. I look away and try to breathe. Get a grip, Amy-Kate!

Another couple walks in as Kyle comes over to me.

"I guess I should have dressed differently," I say, watching the other couple as they purchase entrance to the wine tasting thing. The woman is wearing what might be called an evening gown except it only comes to her knees. It's silver and shimmery. Her heels match and her jewelry is breathtaking, all sparkles and dangles.

I hadn't wanted to jinx the evening by wearing the same outfit I had when Kyle failed to call. So no heels. In fact, my outfit is decidedly casual compared to this woman. My knee-high boots, skinny jeans, and gray turtleneck looked adorable in my room, but now I just feel sloppy and under-dressed.

Kyle looks me up and down, which makes me blush. I tuck my hair behind my ear self-consciously.

"You look wonderful," he says and holds out his arm for me, like we're in Victorian England or something.

I hesitate, not sure exactly what to do. Place my arm on top of his? Hold his arm with my hand? Both hands? I finally thread my arm under his and place my hand on his bicep, and of course, my cheeks color even more at the touch. His arm is firm and steadying. I can feel the heat of him through his shirt and I want to lean into him and soak that heat up. Not that my face needs any more heat.

# Chapter Eleven

WE SPEND THE next two hours walking from room to room, tasting wine in tiny crystal glasses and cheese on silver toothpicks offered by men in tuxedos, and looking at strange artwork. Kyle seems at ease, as if sculptures made of rusted silverware and paintings of dripping circles and squares are his natural habitat.

I myself fail to see how these things count as works of art, much less how they are meant to evoke "longing" or "mistrust" as the plaques beside them claim. One piece of work is a large canvas with trash glued to it.

I give a snort of a laugh when I see it. "Maybe I should take up art," I say. "I could make that in five minutes. You think they would hang my trash on the wall if I donated it here?"

Kyle frowns. "I do concede your point," he says, "but look." He points to the plaque. "The artist was thinking of all the wildlife that are affected by the plastics we throw out. He used artwork as a way to 'lament the state of our planet.'" He stepped back and considered the painting seriously. "I think he is trying to make a serious and valid point."

"Oh." I look at the canvas again, staring at a dirty crushed soda can stuck halfway on the edge like it's going to tumble off. I think of animals coming across this junk and it does kind of make me sad, thinking about it like that. Maybe there is something to this modern art thing after all.

"Okay, I guess I can see it," I say.

Kyle smiles, an expression that lights up his brown eyes and brings out his laugh lines. It makes me want to touch those lines, touch his cheek where a five o'clock shadow is just starting to appear. I swallow and look away.

***

"Did you enjoy yourself?" Kyle asks as we leave the museum, coat and suit coat back on, the outside chill helping to cool my perpetually hot face.

"I did," I say, and am surprised that I mean it. And it wasn't just the company I enjoyed. "I didn't really get a lot of the artwork," I say, "but there were a couple pieces that really spoke to me. Usually after you explained them."

He smiles. "Glad I could be of assistance."

"Thank you for taking me on a date," I say. "Finally."

He dips his head toward me, and his eyes find mine. My heart flutters and I have to focus on not looking away. He holds my gaze as he says, "I really am sorry. I hope you know I would never intentionally hurt you."

I realize his eyes aren't just brown, like I had thought. The setting sun hitting them from the side lights up golden threads looped around his iris. They're breath taking.

We stand there a moment, eyes locked, me with my hands shoved in my coat pockets and Kyle pressing his lips together uncertainly. Is he thinking about kissing me? Am I thinking about kissing him? My eyes dart to his lips and back to his eyes. Yes, I am definitely thinking about kissing those lips now.

My face instantly heats. "I should go!" I say in a rush, taking a step back. "Got to be… somewhere. See you!" I try to pull my hand from my pocket to wave, but the coat sleeve button gets caught in the pocket. I wave my elbow awkwardly instead, blushing like an idiot, and hurry away.

Where on earth did I park? Am I even walking in the right direction?

A car on the street slows down as it passes me and I glance over, wondering if the driver has seen the exchange and is laughing at me. The driver isn't laughing. That's a small relief. I turn away, then frown and look back, but the car is already past. I could have sworn that the driver was that woman from the flower shop. Kyle's ex-fiance. She was wearing sunglasses, but there was no mistaking those larger than life bright red lips. And that hair.

Was she watching us? Stalking us? I think of the serial killer on the news, shiver, and hurry faster.

# Chapter Twelve

I SIT ON THE FLOOR of the flower shop, behind the counter, leaning my back against it, and grinning like an idiot at the text on my phone.

Kyle: Thank you again for such a splendid evening. I hope we can see each other again soon.

He had a wonderful time! He wants to see me again! I sigh dramatically and flop sideways onto the tiles, clutching the phone to my chest like I'm in a soap opera. I remember his eyes locked on mine, the sincerity in them. The gold threaded through the brown of his irises. I let out another contented sigh.

"If you're finally done reading that text and giggling about it, you should come and give me a hand," Mom says. Standing at the counter by my feet, she's working on the corsages for the upcoming wedding.

I heave myself upright. "Just give me a moment," I say, looking over the text again for the dozenth time. "He said he hopes we can see each other again!"

"Yes, so I've heard."

"And he used the word 'splendid!' That's such a Kyle word! Who says that anymore?"

Mom sighs loudly. "Yes, he's incredible and unique and... what was the other word you used?"

"Dreamy? Talented? Kindhearted?"

Mom snorts. "You've known the man two days and yesterday you were decidedly set on calling him a jerk. Forgive me if I have a hard time believing your current assessment of him."

I frown at her and get to my feet. "It was a misunderstanding."

"Mmm-hmm. Here." She slides some flowers over to me and heads for the employees-only door. "Trim off the leaves, would you?"

My phone buzzes and I pounce on it. But it's not Kyle.

Fred: Pizza and games tonight? My place?

I text back, "Sure" and then pull up Kyle's text again to read it just one more time.

"You at least can't deny that he's dreamy," I say loudly, knowing Mom can still hear me in the back room. "You said yourself that he-"

The bell tinkles on the doorway and I freeze, almost ducking behind the counter again. It's Kyle's ex-fiance - Jillian. Guess I'm not the bravest. But it's too late to duck and cover anyway. She's seen me. And her eyes are locked onto me like a cheetah stalking its prey.

The cheetah analogy is especially fitting since she's wearing a leopard or jaguar or some other poor dead cat's fur as a coat. Her hair is just as big as before and as she points one blood red nail at me, I feel like I'm about to be torn apart.

"You!" Jillian spits, clacking her way up to the counter and jamming her finger at me like the barrel of a gun.

"Excuse me?" My voice is a squeak.

"I saw you!" Jillian says, leaning across the counter and jabbing me in the sternum. "I saw you with him! That man is mine!" She says the last word so viciously that her spit hit me in the face.

I wince and turn my head away.

"If you ever come near him again, you'll regret it!" She leans in and I lean back, my feet apparently frozen to the floor, my heart thumping like a cornered rabbit's. Her voice drops. "I can do things your naive little mind has never dreamed of. Make one more move toward him, and I will make you disappear."

My blood goes cold.

"Is there a problem?"

My heart gives a leap of hope. Mom is here.

She stalks over to us, putting herself in front of me, obviously sensing danger to her offspring. I wonder how much of Jillian's threats she heard.

Jillian sizes Mom up.

I wonder who will win in this fight: angry cheetah or mama bear. I'm betting on the mama bear. Having her here in full protector mode is kind of comforting.

"Yes, there's a problem," Jillian says. "She is a dirty, man-stealing &$@*$!"

Uh oh. Mom's face takes on a storm-like quality I recognize. No one, absolutely no one, gets away with swearing in front of Mom.

"How dare you," Mom says, coming around the counter and facing down the woman. "I will not let you come into my shop and swear at my daughter! Leave now, or I will call the authorities!"

"Your daughter?" she asks. "Did she learn how to steal men from you?" The anger coming from her is almost visible, charging the air like electricity before a storm.

"This is your last warning," Mom says. "Leave the premises!"

I cower behind the counter, feeling pathetic and intimidated by both of these ferocious women. I'm not ferocious. I don't have a wild animal side that can take on a predator. I feel like a little bird, holding perfectly still and hoping I'll go unnoticed long enough to get away. I've never been good at confrontation.

"Fine!" the woman says. "But keep your daughter under control!" She turns on her tall heels and stalks out of the shop.

The door slams behind her with a tinkle of bells that doesn't fit the mood at all. Mom and I stand still for a moment.

"Well!" Mom turns toward me, still blazing.

I step back, afraid her anger is now directed at me for some reason.

"Don't you let that woman scare you!" Mom says, pointing her finger at me. "You have just as much right to like that man as she does! You are twice the woman she will ever be and don't you dare let her make you feel inferior! You hear me?"

My eyes go wide and I nod.

"Mark my words, there is something wrong with that woman. I can see it in her eyes."

I swallow and remember my serial killer theory. I was mostly joking before about Jillian being a murderer, but maybe there is something to it. I shiver, remembering her threat. That definitely sounded like something a creepy serial killer would say.

I will make you disappear.

I swallow.

"Coming in here and cursing you out!" Mom mutters, turning away. "Who does she think she is? I have half a mind to call the cops on her anyways." She keeps muttering as she pushes through the employees only door, shaking her head.

I exhale a shaky breath. What have I gotten myself into?

# Chapter Thirteen

"WHAT IS THAT?" I ask, as Fred opens the back of his car to reveal an enormous flat cardboard box. It's roughly three feet wide.

"Pizza!" he says. "I told you I would pick us up a pizza!"

"That is not a pizza," I say, as he slides it out. But the box does have a picture of pizza on it. And it smells heavenly.

"Grab the other side, would you?" he asks.

As we heft the monstrosity out of the car, I say, "We're going to have to turn it sideways to fit it through the door! Where did you find this thing? It looks like it got hit with an enlarging ray!"

He laughs. "You've never had giant pizza before?"

"I've had an extra-large, but this is obese! You could fit a child in this box! A very flat child."

As we reach his front door, he balances his end of the pizza box in one hand as he fishes in his pocket for his keys. I feel my phone buzz and pull it out of my pocket and light up the screen one-handed. My heart leaps when I see Kyle's name on the screen.

Kyle: Would you like to accompany me on a date tomorrow evening? I feel I still owe you an outing to the King's Valley Restaurant. Would six o'clock suit you?

I'm grinning like an idiot as I maneuver the phone in my hand to be able to text back with just my thumb.

Me: You don't owe me anything. But six o'clock would be perfect!

"Good news?" Fred asks.

I look up to see he's got the door open and is waiting for me.

"Yeah. Sorry." I stuff my phone back in my pocket and try to reign in my smile as I follow him inside.

I'm always happy to hang out with Fred, but I can't lie. I'd rather be with Kyle.

Fred's apartment is always surprisingly clean. Cleaner than my apartment anyway. You'd think from his casual appearance that he wouldn't be bothered to do much cleaning. But the place is always nice. We've been friends something like fifteen years now, and it was the same when we were in high school. His room was always tidy when I came over. But right now, his apartment isn't just tidy, it's like he did some serious deep-cleaning. I can still smell the chemical lemon scent of glass cleaner. I guess he was in a germ-killing mood recently.

His front room is furnished with a big comfy leather couch against the far wall, a coffee table with an over-sized book full of photographs of space, and several posters on the wall from his t-shirt company. One has two atoms talking to each other, and another has elements from the periodical table lined up to spell "Ge Ni U S." A large flat-screen TV is against one wall on a low table with X-Box controllers beside it.

"This is nice," I say, sliding off my shoes. I usually leave them on, but the amount of cleanliness in here makes taking them off seem the thing to do.

He shrugs. "You don't have to take off your shoes. This carpet has seen much worse! As you well know!"

"This place is too clean to wear shoes in!"

"You do whatever you feel like doing," he says.

"Yeah? What if I feel like jumping on your couch and throwing pepperoni everywhere?"

He bursts out laughing. "Then do it!"

"Even in your sparkling clean apartment?"

"I cleaned it for you," he says, still laughing. "If you prefer it messy, by all means, make it feel more like home!"

I give a single breath of a laugh. "Well, all right then. Lucky for you, I don't actually feel like doing that. I'm more the sit on the couch and eat the pizza kind of gal."

"Whew!" says Fred. "Glad my best friend isn't secretly a pepperoni throwing maniac!" He grins.

He balances the giant pizza on the side of the coffee table and then slides the outer-space book beneath the table to make enough room for it.

"I'll grab plates," he says, standing. "Want anything to drink?"

"Just some water. Thanks."

"Cool. You can check out the board games in the coat closet if you want! Be right back!"

I feel weirdly self-conscious, standing there in my stocking feet. The carpet is obviously newly vacuumed with lines still showing. He vacuumed for me. This isn't a date, right? Because I'm definitely almost dating Kyle and I don't want to mess that up.

I curl my toes. There isn't much to be done about that now. I'll just have to throw in some comments about what a great friend Fred is, emphasis on friend. He did just call me his best friend, so that's a good sign, right?

I head for the coat closet and am almost crushed to death when I open the door. Several board games fall out and I let out a squeak as I jump back.

"You all right?" Fred asks, coming back into the room with two plastic cups of water and some paper plates tucked under his arm.

"Your games just tried to murder me!"

He laughs. "Nah. They're friendly. They're just excited someone might play them!"

"I have my doubts."

He sets everything on top of the pizza box and comes over to the closet. "Let's see here. What jumped out at you? Battleship Arena?"

"No way! You get seriously competitive with that one."

"Okay, okay. Spark Night? Oh, here's Mountain Adventure! I love this game! We haven't played this in forever! No wonder it threw itself at you. It must be a little desperate."

I laugh. "I know the type."

"Want to play? It's cooperative so my competitiveness will work in your favor."

"Fine. But don't we usually lose? I think it's because I jinx it. Remember in high school how in sports I was labeled as bad luck because whatever team I was on lost. Without fail. You sure you want to risk it?"

He gives a mischievous grin. "Oh, bring it on!"

I laugh.

# Chapter Fourteen

AN HOUR LATER, we've barely made a dent in the massive pizza and our lives are on the line. At least, our characters' lives.

"We're going to win if I have to drag you up this mountain Samwise style!" Fred says, furiously shaking the dice in his cupped hands. He throws them down into the top of the game box where they rattle and come to rest on a one and a two.

"Seriously?" He puts his face in his hands. "Why? Why do the dice hate me?"

"I told you," I say, grabbing the dice. "It's the curse of my bad luck."

"Shhh!" Fred puts his finger to my lips. I start away from him. Is he flirting with me? "Don't say that!" he whispers. "If you think you can or you think you can't, you're right! Abraham Lincoln."

I shake my head. "Show off." I shake the dice but he puts his hand over the box before I can tip them in.

"Repeat after me," he says. "We are going to win this game!"

I roll my eyes. "What is this, a magical spell?"

"Just do it! Prove old Abe right! We are going to win this game!"

I sigh. "We are going to win this game," I say in a deadpan.

He nods solemnly and withdraws his hand. I dump the dice them into the box. A five and a two.

"Yes!" Fred and I say in unison, with me punching the air and him jumping all the way out of his seat.

"We did it!" I move my character proudly up the last space of the mountain, claiming the treasure.

"I knew you could do it!" Fred says, and pulls me to him, hugging me.

I tense at the closeness and he lets go. He hasn't hugged me since we were kids. And, weirdly, it was kind of nice.

He's grinning from ear to ear. "The curse is broken! The bad luck is banished! You are free!"

I laugh and flop backward, spreading out my arms on the couch behind me.

"Good old Abe was right!" says Fred.

"I don't think he'd want you calling him old," I point out.

"He'd be like 200 years old at this point," says Fred. "That qualifies as old no matter what definition you're using."

"Nerd."

He laughs and sits back down next to me. I move my arm, conscious of how close he is, to make sure it doesn't accidentally brush against him. Am I being weird? I think I'm being weird around him.

We sit in comfortable silence a few minutes, until I decide to voice what's been on my mind all day.

"You know that story that's all over the news?"

He frowns. "I thought you don't watch the news."

"I don't! Not if I can help it. But when I was at the coffee shop the other day, this lady next to me was listening to the news with the volume turned way up. Seriously, I think she was deaf or something."

"Was it about all those dead rich guys?" Fred asks.

I nod. "So creepy! And, I know this is ridiculous, but I have a theory about who the serial killer might be."

Fred's eyebrows shoot up. "Wait, really?"

"It's just a theory and it's probably nothing, but you know that guy who stood me up on Valentine's Day?"

A storm cloud enters Fred's eyes. "The jerk who came into the flower shop with his fiance?"

"Yes!" I nod vigorously.

"But it can't be a dude. The serial killer is a girl who poses as-" His eyes widen. "Oh! You think it's his fiance!"

"Exactly!"

He considers this. "I mean, she did seem a little weird."

"Kyle - that guy - he came to the flower shop as I was closing up that night-"

"Wait, what? Are you okay? What did he want?"

"I'm fine!" I hold up my hands to placate him. "He just wanted to apologize. He explained that Jillian, that woman, is actually his ex-finace. He broke it off with her like a month ago but she's pretending like they're still together and everything is just fine."

Fred is glowering. "Did he ask you out again?"

"That doesn't matter," I say, waving his question away with my hand, but I know my pink cheeks have given away the answer. "The point is, I asked if she had been written into his will, and he said yes!"

Fred is still frowning.

"Also," I plow ahead, wondering if it was a bad idea to bring this up at all. "Jillian came into the shop today, by herself, and she was so mad. She yelled at me and cussed at me about stealing her man and threatened me and everything. I think she is legit crazy."

"She threatened you? Seriously? What did she say?"

I can remember her words exactly, along with the chill I got from them. "She said that if I didn't leave Kyle alone, I would regret it."

"Everyone says stuff like that though."

"Yeah, but then she said that she could do things I would never dream of. I got the sense it was like do bad things, obviously. She said if I made another move toward Kyle that she would make me disappear."

Fred's eyebrows shoot up. "That's freaky! Did you call the cops or something?"

"No, it's fine. My mom was there and she handled it."

"So she heard her threaten you?"

"Well, no, she was in the back during that part. I didn't tell her because I didn't want to worry her. But she agrees that there is something wrong with Jillian. She said her eyes were kind of crazy-looking."

Fred's gaze on me is intense.

I look away and keep going, wanting to get everything out there, to get his opinion. "I really think it might be her! I mean, maybe. It could be! Also-" I break off. I was about to tell him about seeing Jillian in her car, watching me, after my date with Kyle, but I don't know how to bring that up without talking about the date itself. And that seems like a bad idea. "Also, I saw her watching me the other day," I say. "She drove past me in her car, really slowly, and was looking at me."

"That's creepy," says Fred.

"I know! Like, serial killer creepy, right?"

Fred contemplates this for a moment. "If it really might be her, then we should tell the police."

I lean back into the couch. "Except it's just a theory. I

don't have any actual proof."

"True... But threatening you is a pretty big deal. You should at least report that."

"You think?"

He nods. "And I'd stay away from this Kyle guy. I mean, it's not his fault if he's being targeted by a crazy lady, but it seems like it would be a lot safer to stay far away from both of them."

"Hmmm," I say, not really willing to commit to that. Like he said, it's not Kyle's fault. And anyways, if there's a killer after him, shouldn't someone warn him?

"Yeah, I guess I should call the police. I just don't want to worry Mom, and what if the police want to ask her questions or something?"

"You mom's tough," he says. "She can handle it."

"Yeah. Okay." I fish my phone out of my pocket. "You've convinced me."

I dial the non-emergency police number.

"Police station. How can I direct your call?" a male voice asks.

"Uh, I want to report a suspicious person?" I glance at Fred who nods encouragingly at me.

"One moment," the man says.

A moment later a woman's voice comes on the line. "This is Officer Rhodes. What can I do for you?"

My hand is sweating. I don't know why I'm so nervous.

I'm not the serial killer!

"I, uh, want to report someone," I say, clutching the phone to my ear. "A woman. Her name is Jillian Lynch."

The woman sighs like she gets this sort of call all the time and is so over it. "What about her is suspicious exactly?"

"Uh, she threatened me."

"Threatened you?"

I swallow. "Yeah, she came into my mom's shop where I was and cussed at me and told me to stay away from this guy or she would make me regret it."

"Stay away from a guy?"

"Uh, yeah. She used to be dating - well, engaged, actually - to this guy and now I'm-" I break off and glance at Fred. "Uh, and she saw me with him and got mad I guess."

"Hmm. Is that all?" She sounds bored.

Is that all? "When she threatened me, she said she'd make me disappear. Like, I got the feeling she was saying she was going to, like, kill me, you know?"

"Mmm-hmm. Those were her exact words?"

"Yes."

"All right, I'll make a note. Anything else?"

"Uh." I glance at Fred who nods vigorously, but I don't know what else to say. I suddenly feel foolish. Nothing she has done has been illegal. And this woman seems to think this is just about some guy. I press on anyway.

"She seems, um, unstable."

"How so?" the woman asks.

"She just- um…" I have no idea how to explain this. She has a crazy look in her eyes sometimes? "I saw her in her car the other day."

Silence. "Yes?"

"Like, I was out, and she was in her car, and I think she was following me."

The officer sighs again and I feel my face getting red. I can't explain things the right way. She isn't taking this seriously.

"I've made a note. Do you want to file a complaint against her?" she asks.

"No, I just-" I bite my lip, but I might as well get everything out there. "I think she might be the serial killer," I say in a rush. "The one from the news who killed all those rich guys. She was dating this guy who is definitely rich and she asked to be written into his will and then she threatened me-" I break off. That's really all there is. "So, I just thought you should, you know, look into her. Just in case."

There is a silence on the other end, and I wonder if she might finally be taking this seriously. Then the woman says. "Thank you for your concern, ma'am, but there are detectives handling that case. Have a good day." The line goes dead.

# Chapter Fifteen

"WHAT DID SHE SAY?" Fred asks as I lower the phone from my ear.

I shake my head. "I should have had you call. She'd have listened to you."

Fred frowns. "I guess we don't have any actual evidence, but I think the only evidence we're going to get is a dead guy!"

"Ugh." I put my face in my hand. "Maybe she isn't the serial killer! Maybe I'm wrong about this!" Maybe I'm just jealous, I think.

Fred puts a hand on my shoulder. "Hey," he says. "Don't give up. I believe you." His hand is warm and solid. I want him to keep it there, but he takes it away much too soon.

"Maybe," he says slowly, "you should mention this to Kyle. If you have a way to contact him."

I swallow, feeling strangely guilty. "Uh, yeah. Okay. That's a good idea."

"Just so he can be on his guard," Fred says.

I nod and wonder why the thought of Fred finding out I have been on a few dates with Kyle bothers me. He wouldn't be jealous, would he? No, probably just concerned for my safety after what I just told him. Do I want him to be jealous?

I shove the thought away.

Fred's eyes light up and a mischievous grin plays on his lips.

"Wait, wait, wait," I say. "I know that look. That look has gotten us into trouble way too many times!"

He laughs. "I was just thinking, if you're so sure about this, why don't we get some proof?"

"Like, the two of us? Being, what, detectives or something?"

He nods eagerly and goes to his desk to grab a notebook and pen.

I shake my head. "We barely won our board game! We'd never be able to find clues and proof and things like that. Well, you probably could, but I'd just drag you down. Bad luck, remember?"

He shakes his head and sits back down next to me, opening the notebook to a fresh page. "We just broke the spell!"

I roll my eyes. "It's probably not even her. She's just a desperate woman who wishes she was still engaged to an insanely rich man."

"But it adds up, you know," Fred says. "Just like you said. It might not be her, but what if it is and we don't do anything?"

"Didn't you just say we should stay away from her?"

"That was before the police didn't take it seriously," says Fred. He uncaps the pen and writes How to Save a Rich Guy From Being Murdered across the top of the page. He has good handwriting.

I bite my lip. I just wanted to talk about it with him, not actually do anything to stop a murderer! "I don't know. I really don't think I'm up to it. I'd probably botch it and end up dead too or something."

"Amy-Kate." Fred looks at me with such intensity that I look away and start fiddling with my game piece.

"You are one of the most capable people I know." His voice is so serious, not joking and playful like usual. "You could take on the world if you wanted to."

I give a snort. It sounds derisive. I can't help it. "This was just a game, Fred."

"I know. I'm not talking about the game."

I glance at him and he's still giving me that intense look, like he's trying to imprint something into my mind.

"So why would you say something like that?"

"Because I'm not sure you know it. And it's true."

My cheeks go pink. I pull the box toward me and start putting the game pieces back, one at a time.

When I glance at him again, he's still giving me an intense stare and I realize a second later that he's purposely overdoing it, making his eyes wide, trying to get me to laugh.

I oblige and the tension breaks.

"You'd better eat more pizza," he says, settling back on the couch. "Or it's never going to fit in my fridge!"

I laugh and help myself to another piece. "Okay, you've convinced me. What do you have in mind? Please tell me it's nothing illegal! I don't want to be the one who ends up in jail at the end of this."

Fred clears this throat. "Step one," he says and writes it down. "We need to gather intelligence. Gather intel on the suspect." He draws a little magnifying glass next to step one. His pen strokes are so fast and sure, just like everything else about him. I wish I was more like that.

"So, like Facebook stalk her?" I ask.

"Yes!" he says, pointing the pen at me. "Good idea! We'll start with online info, since that will be the easiest to get. He adds the word online to step one. "So step two will be, interrogate the victim."

I choke on my pizza. "Interrogate? You mean Kyle?" I picture Kyle tied to a chair with a single light bulb dangling over his head. "Why are we interrogating him? Why not Jillian?"

"If you get a chance to talk to Jillian, feel free to question her, but I think it's going to be tricky to get her alone."

That is a good point.

"I can do that step," I say. "By myself." I try to sound confidant, but really, I just don't want Fred and Kyle talking to each other. That would just be way too weird.

"Okay," says Fred, sketching a face that looks remarkably like Kyle's next to step two. "So then, step three." He taps his lips with the pen. "What do you think step three should be?"

I shrug. "Ask other people. I don't know if Jillian is from around here, but we could see if anyone else knows about her."

"Good idea." He writes reconnaissance next to step three and draws some speech bubbles. "And if we're still unsure at that point-" He writes step four - spy. "We'll take matters into our own hands!"

I shake my head. "I think you are way too excited about this."

He grins. "And then, the last step will be to take the evidence to the police, of course." He draws a little police badge next to the last step. "Once we have enough evidence, they'll have to believe us."

"I sure hope so!"

"So are we doing this?" Fred asks.

I take a deep breath. "We're doing this."

# Chapter Sixteen

STEP ONE IS TO Internet stalk Jillian, or 'gather intel' as Fred said.

So as soon as I get home from Fred's, I boot up my computer and hop online. I type her name into the search bar and hit enter. A bunch of stuff comes up about some random singer woman named Jillian Linch, but with a different spelling of her last name. And this singer woman is clearly not the Jillian that threatened me in my mom's flower shop. Singer Jillian has pink hair and a butterfly tattoo on her cheek. I scroll, but find nothing. Even when I change my search to exclude the different spelling of "Linch," there's still nothing on Jillian. One doctor at a hospital in Main comes up - a Jill Lynch. There's a picture. She's African American. There's also a blog written by a patriotic chicken farmer named James Lynch who posts pictures of chickens wearing cowboy hats and bandannas. I end up watching three cat videos by someone named jillion079 before I shake myself and close out of them. I don't even like cats!

I open up social media and try finding a profile. There are several Jillain Lynch's who even spell their name the same, but none of the photos look like her. One profile just features a cartoon of a banana as their profile picture, but it says they live in Canada. This is going nowhere.

I know I'm no expert at finding people online, but surely something should come up. I finally go to a website that claims they can find people for you and even give you their address, phone number, and criminal record, for only $10. It's a sign of how desperate I am that I shell out the cash.

I put in her name, our county, and a range for her birth year. She looks about my age, but I give it a whole decade to search through.

I hold my breath as it searches.

But when the results come back, they've found nothing. Not a single thing.

I frown and expand the date range for her birthday. Maybe she's older than she looks? Or maybe Kyle likes younger women? Still nothing. I expand the area, thinking maybe she lives out of the county. But still nothing. In the entire state, there is one woman named Jillian Lynch with the proper spelling. She's 87 years old.

I groan and push back from the computer. That was $10 down the drain. Maybe if I got some solid information about her, it would be easier to search. Like a phone number or address.

I wonder if I could borrow Kyle's phone - assuming I see him again - and take a peek at his contacts. If I had her phone number, maybe I could track her down that way. It's worth a shot. And step two is to "interrogate the victim" anyway. I blush at the thought. How on earth am I going to pull that off without sounding like a paranoid weirdo?

A yawn pushes it's way out my mouth. I glance at the clock. It's 2am! Good grief. I spent more time on those cat videos than I thought.

Promising myself that I will get to the bottom of this, I climb into bed, still fully clothed, and fall asleep.

# Chapter Seventeen

THIS IS IT. The date that should have happened on Valentine's Day. I stand inside the entrance to the restaurant, feeling a weird sense of Deja-vu. Is Kyle actually going to show up this time? The hostesses at the desk are different than the ones who worked the shift on Valentine's Day, thank goodness. I don't think I'd be able to stand there and wait a second time with the same pitying eyes on me.

I tug self-consciously at the new dress I'm wearing. I felt so out of place on our last date that I decided to splurge a little - okay, a lot - and buy a nice dress. Like, a really nice dress. I asked around on some fashion groups on social media for ideas, since I am very ignorant when it comes to fashion. A lot of their recommendations were a little too wild for me. I guess trendy fashion often involves strange dresses that are missing half the fabric they should have, revealing stomachs and backs and shoulders and such. In the end, I decided on a dress that was comparatively tame but that everyone assured me was the top of the line.

I ordered it online since I didn't have the guts to walk into a high end dress shop in my jeans and hoodie. When it arrived, it was wrapped like a present and nestled in tissue paper. It was so fragile feeling that I was afraid I would tear it. There's a reason I don't own many fancy clothes. I tend to forget what I'm wearing and do something like wipe my hands on my clothes and get dirt all over them.

But as I pulled the dress from the box, I had to admit this piece of clothing was more like art than regular clothes. It was knee length, with the hem cut at a slant. Around the shoulders was an extra piece of cloth cut in an opposite diagonal leaving the shoulders exposed. It reminded me of the modern art we had looked at, which was one of the reasons I chose it. Could I really wear this?

Now, here I stand, in a golden silk piece of art, trying to look like I match it. And wondering how I am going to sneak questions about Jillian into this date. Just the thought makes the butterflies in my stomach triple.

Then I see Amanda. And I thought I couldn't feel any more nervous. She pushes through the restaurant double door, chatting with her two friends, of course. Lola and Lala or whatever their names are.

My first instinct is to duck behind a potted plant and pray she doesn't see me. But that's stupid. I have as much right to be here as she does. And this dress isn't the sort to be subjected to ducking. So I hold my ground. But as her glance snags on me, I inwardly cringe. Her gaze is scrutinizing. Calculating. She strides straight for me.

"Amy!" she says, her voice all bright in a way that doesn't match her eyes. "How funny seeing you here! I didn't know you came to this restaurant!"

I give a weak smile, straightening my spine and trying to look like I belong. I tug at the dress, worried that I don't know how to wear it right. "Oh, I'm just meeting someone here," I say, waving my hand airily like this is an everyday occurrence.

Amanda raises her eyebrows. "How exciting." She takes in my dress and her eyebrows rise higher. "Is that a Les Cardone?"

"Oh, wow!" says one of her friends. Layla? "It's so pretty! It makes your eyes stand out. Good choice!"

I blush faintly. "Thank you." Are they seriously admiring my outfit? This is a first. I guess the fashion groups were right.

"Who are you meeting?" asks Amanda.

"Uh, well…" I stall, not sure how to answer. My boyfriend? We aren't official yet.

"Amy-Kate!"

A wave of relief washes over me almost making my knees buckle. He came!

Kyle strides into the restaurant in his classic outfit with the blue suit jacket open and the white shirt unbuttoned at his throat. I swear he gets more handsome every time I see him.

"Kyle!" I move toward him like being pulled by a magnet.

"Sorry I'm late," he says, giving me a quick side hug. He hugged me! Squee! "Traffic was a nightmare." He takes in my dress and smiles. "You clean up very well." Then he looks over at Amanda and her cronies. "Friends of yours?"

Sort of. "This is Amanda," I say. "And... Lola and Layla," I add quickly gesturing at both of them at once and praying I got at least one of their names right. "And this is Kyle."

Kyle gives a small chuckle, and he almost sounds nervous. I glance at him, but he only holds out a hand. "Ladies, it is a pleasure." He shakes each of their hands in turn and Lona or Layna or whatever their names are both beam. "I'm glad you could keep my Amy-Kate company. I hate to keep her waiting."

His Amy-Kate? My cheeks warm with pleasure and I stand a little taller.

"Oh, the pleasure was all ours," Amanda gushes. "We've been friends with Amy-Kate here since high school you know."

I swear this is the first time I've ever heard her use my full name. Amazing how having a guy like Kyle is such a game changer!

"Is that so?" he asks. "How wonderful! It's so good to keep in touch with good friends over the years. You must be very close."

I almost snort, but catch myself.

Amanda smiles. "In fact, Amy-Kate, dear. I was just going to invite you to lunch tomorrow. Are you free?"

My mouth hangs open. Literally. "Lunch?"

"Oh yes," she says. "You simply must come."

"Why that would be lovely," says Kyle. "I'm sure Amy-Kate would love to come, wouldn't you?"

I blink. "Uh, I guess so?" Why do I sound like such an idiot?

Amanda grins a sweet smile. It's the most genuine-looking smile I have ever seen her give me. "Does noon work?"

I nod, mutely.

She claps her hands. "Oh, wonderful! You'll love it! I'll text you with more info."

"We'd better grab a seat," says Kyle. "I can only stay for an hour, so we'd better make this a spectacular hour! Ladies." He nods to them and ushers me to the hostesses.

# Chapter Eighteen

WE'RE SEATED IN a little booth beside a trickling stone water fountain. I try not to stare. There are plants everywhere - trees in pots against the walls, ivy hanging from the ceiling, and a huge twisting tree growing right up from the ground in the center of the restaurant. Judging from the fresh earthy smell, they are all real. The waiters wear tuxedos and someone is playing a grand piano beside the big tree. The ceiling is painted to look like a sunset with pink clouds and a yellow sky.

"This looks like how I imagine heaven," I say.

Kyle chuckles. He doesn't seem to give many outright laughs, but his chuckle is deep and rich. I like the sound of it.

"Glad I could bring you here then," Kyle smiles at me in such a soft sweet way that I look down at the menu in a desperate attempt to keep my blush from spreading.

"Order whatever you would like," Kyle says.

I finally take in what I'm looking at and my mouth falls open. Again. It's happening a lot today.

I'd been right about the prices. It would be a couple day's wages for me to pay for a meal here. I close my mouth and swallow. Now probably isn't the best time to ask what he does for work. But oh my heavens he does something lucrative.

Most of the menu items I can't pronounce so I have to rely on the descriptions, which included things like "imported from Holland," "aged at least twenty-five years," and "only found off the coast of Africa." Some of the things I can understand, like quail, caviar, and lobster. None of them sound particularly appetizing since I'm not a seafood kind of gal and the thought of eating cute little birds doesn't sit well with me.

"What are you getting?" I ask, desperate for some guidance in this mess of foreign words and hefty price tags.

"I think I'll have the-" And then he sneezes.

"Bless you," I say.

He chuckles. "That's the name of the dish."

I color. "Oh. That sounds… appetizing."

"It really is! You should try it!"

"I'm not a big fan of seafood," I say.

He smiles. "It's not seafood."

"Oh."

"If you don't like seafood, you could try the fois gras."

"Uh, alright. Where's that?"

He points and the word "liver" stands out in the description. I try to make a polite face, but I think he notices me gag. "What else would you recommend?"

I finally settle on a chicken dish. With regular chicken meat, not the one with chicken hearts. Shudder. One heart is enough inside of me, thank you. Chicken is something I can eat. As long as they don't do anything too weird to it.

"How's your day been?" I ask, when the tuxedoed waiter takes our menus away.

He leans back in his chair. "It's been rather long. How is your day going?"

I shrug, trying to think of something to talk about. "Pretty good. I helped my mom in the flower shop."

"That's wonderful! I'm glad you have a hobby you enjoy so much!"

I nod. Is it just a hobby? Silence settles between us and I listen to the peaceful piano music. This is a place I would like to come take a nap in, not eat strange food. But I figure appreciating the ambiance is as good a thing to do as any.

"Oh," says Kyle. "I almost forgot! I bought you something!"

I grin. "Really?"

Smiling, he reaches into his pocket, pulling out a small silver jewelry box tied with a thin ribbon. For a second my heart stops, like I think it's going to be a ring inside. But that's ridiculous.

"Are you sure?" I ask, but I'm already taking the box from him.

"It's my pleasure," he says. "When I saw this it made me think of you, and I had to get it. I just know you'll love it!"

I untie the ribbon and pop the box open to find a set of earrings sitting in black velvet. My breath catches. "These are beautiful!"

They are two lilies, set with mother of pearl and a real pearl in the center of each. "I love them!" They're almost too beautiful too touch, shimmering and ethereal.

"I know how much you love flowers," he says. "And these are almost as beautiful as you."

I don't think it's possible to stop blushing in his presence. When I sneak a glance at him, he's beaming, his eyes lit up like nothing pleases him more than to see me so happy.

"I want to wear them right now," I say, taking out my current earrings which are cheap little fake pearls.

"Here," says Kyle. "Allow me." He leans over the table and gently lifts the first lily earring from me, then takes my earlobe between his fingers.

His fingers are steady and warm. It's strangely intimate, and I know my blush is nearing danger levels. He slides the earring in without any trouble and affixes the backing, then moves to my other ear. When both earrings are in, he doesn't pull his hand away. Instead, he cups the side of my face with his palm.

"Beautiful," he murmurs, and when I dare to look at him, he's looking at me, not the earring. His gaze slides to my lips. I inhale. Is he going to kiss me? Right here? Right now?

"I have a fois gras," says a waiter and I jump back.

"Fois gras? I believe there's been a mistake," Kyle says, cool as anything. "We didn't order the fois gras."

"Oh, sorry!" says the waiter. He looks young, maybe just out of high school. "It's my first day. Yours must be the chicken cordon blu."

"I think so?" I say.

Kyle nods and the waiter places the dish in front of me. "I'll be back with yours in just a moment, sir." With an awkward bow, the waiter leaves.

"Poor guy," I say, not meeting Kyle's eyes. "I would hate working as a waiter."

"Do you like your current job?" Kyle asks, leaning back in his seat and resting that steady gaze on me.

He's just asking about my job and I'm blushing! I'm hopeless. But I can't stop thinking about his hand on my cheek and his eyes on my lips. What if that waiter hadn't shown up right then?

"Uh, it's alright," I say, fiddling with my fork.

"You're welcome to start eating if you'd like to," Kyle says. "Don't wait on account of me."

On account of me? Who talks like that? It's awesome.

"It's all right," I say. "I'll wait." Actually, I'm a little nervous to see what this things tastes like. I set the fork down.

"Tell me more about yourself," he says. "What do you enjoy doing? What fills your heart with joy?"

"Uh, joy?" I scrunch my forehead. When was the last time my heart had felt 'filled with joy'? I think of winning the board game with Fred yesterday. That was pretty awesome. "I like playing games. Like, board games."

"That sounds nice. We should play together sometime."

I blink. The thought of Kyle sitting on my couch in his suit coat and playing a board game on my coffee table seems strangely out of place. "Uh, yeah. Sure."

"What else do you enjoy?"

I have to think of something else too? "I like… uh… walking?" Why do I always sound like an idiot when I'm around him? "I mean, going on walks. Like, outside and stuff." Could I sound less eloquent? I want to face palm. Instead, my hand starts fiddling with the fork again.

"Please," Kyle says. "You may eat. I insist."

I drop the fork. "It's really fine."

He looks concerned. Probably for my intelligence.

"You enjoy spending time in nature?" he asks.

"Yes!" I say, relieved he found a way to make it sound less pathetic. "I do! I like to pick wildflowers and arrange them." I don't tell him I also like to pretend I'm arranging my own wedding bouquet. The hothouse grown flowers at Mom's shop are gorgeous, but I've always preferred wildflowers myself. Simple. Nothing to brag about maybe. But beautiful in their own way.

Kyle nods and gestures for me to continue. "Please go on. What else do you enjoy about nature?"

I shrug. "All of it, I guess. I like watching the little squirrels and the birds. They're so cute! Oh! One time I saw this mama squirrel that was so huge she was almost fatter sideways than she was tall! She looked like she was going to pop out babies any second!" That came out wrong. I blush and laugh awkwardly.

Kyle gives an obliging chuckle. "You seem to be very observant."

Kyle's phone on the table vibrates. We both looked down at it as Jillian's name shows up bright and clear.

# Chapter Nineteen

MY STOMACH CLENCHES and I remember step two.

"Uh, do you need to take that?" I ask as Kyle's phone keeps at its insistent buzzing, moving a little across the tabletop.

Kyle silences the phone and turns it face down. "Absolutely not," he says. "I am here to spend time with you."

I smile, but it isn't genuine. I pick up my water and take a sip just to have something to do.

"So, uh. Why is Jillian calling you?" I ask. "Does she call often?" I try to keep my voice casual, my eyes on the water glass I'm now spinning slowly in its condensation circle on the table. I'm only asking because I need to interrogate him for information. That's the only reason.

Kyle sighs. "It's undoubtedly about something of hers I need to return to her. It almost feels as though this is a divorce, the way she is dividing things up between mine and hers."

I frown. "Have you ever been divorced?"

"Oh, goodness, no! It's just how I imagine it might be."

That's a relief.

"It's unpleasant," he says. "But I understand. For example, while we were dating I bought her an apartment next door to mine and-"

"You bought her an apartment?" I blink at him.

"Well, yes. The commute to her apartment was through awful traffic and I don't have much free time as you know, and so it was more convenient to have her move next door."

I stare. And keep staring. "Wait, does she still live next door to you?"

He frowns. "Unfortunately. The lease is in her name so I can't terminate it."

My stomach tightens. Kyle must read my expression because he reaches over and takes my hand. "It's not something you need to worry about. Trust me."

His chocolate eyes are so warm, I feel myself start melting.

He squeezes my hand and lets go, but I wish he wouldn't.

"However, she is insisting I continue to pay rent for her since her current rent is more than her old rent was, and it's my fault - her words - that she lives there now."

"So she should just move!" There's more venom in my voice than I intend.

He nods. "I have proposed that to her and she refuses." He lets out another sigh. I feel like the calm exterior he always has is cracking, showing the stress underneath. He rubs the back of his neck. "I think she's just scared of being alone. Which I can understand."

I raise my eyebrows. "It sounds to me like she was just dating you for your money."

"Perhaps," Kyle concedes, folding his hands and resting them on the table.

"What do you do for work anyway?" I ask.

He gives a small smile, looking down at the table for a moment, like he is contemplating. Then he looks up and says, "I work for Isomo as well."

"Oh! I didn't know that. What do you do for them?"

He takes a sip of water. "Honestly, it feels like all I do is attend meetings, but probably everyone feels like that." He chuckles.

I nod. "Right?"

A silence descends, and it feels a little strained. But then the waiter arrives again.

"I have a-" he sneezes. I stifle a laugh.

"Thank you," says Kyle, leaning back so the waiter can place a steaming dish of… something in front of him.

The waiter looks relieved that he's gotten the right order to the right table. "Let me know if you need anything else, okay?" he says. "Oh, and my name is Juan." He points to his name tag. "Enjoy your meal!"

"Thank you," says Kyle.

The waiter leaves and I eye my chicken warily.

"If you don't enjoy it," Kyle says, reading my expression, "we can order something else."

"Oh, no. This is fine!" I don't want to go through that nightmare of a menu again looking for something else edible. Determined, I grab my fork and knife and cut off a chunk. The inside drips with white sauce. The smell at least is good. I steel myself and pop it in my mouth.

"What do you think?" Kyle asks, watching me curiously.

"It's delicious!" And it's true! I dig in with enthusiasm.

Kyle smiles. "I'm so pleased." He picks up his own fork and begins helping himself to small, almost delicate, bites of his dish.

Watching him, I slow down devouring my food, trying to mimic his small bites and pretend I'm a dainty fashionable lady. It takes a lot of imagination.

I eye his phone again, an idea sneaking into my mind. Maybe it's a terrible idea. Or maybe it's brilliant.

I look around the restaurant first to make sure Juan the waiter isn't near by. "It's good," I say, clutching my fork a little too hard. "But it could use a little more salt."

"Of course!" Kyle looks around for a waiter, but, of course, there isn't one near by. "Let me find someone for you." He wipes his mouth on his napkin and stands. "I'll be right back."

Score.

I watch him walk away, heart pounding, and then reach for his phone. It has a passcode, of course. But there is a notification, aside from the missed call from Jillian which doesn't have her phone number, just her name.

Appointment Reminder: Meet Jillian on Saturday, 2:30pm.

That's tomorrow. My stomach squeezes. Why is he meeting her? Is it a date?

Frowning, I tap on the emergency option at the bottom of the screen and find Kyle's medical information. My cheeks heat as I realize how private this is. But it's the only thing I can access without a pass-code! He was born on August 19th, 30 years ago. His blood type is A+. There aren't any medical conditions listed, but there is an emergency contact. My heart sinks a little. It's Jillian. Of course.

He probably had her has his emergency contact when there were engaged and just forgot to change it, I tell myself.

As annoying as that is, it means her phone number is listed right there. I look around for a pen to jot it down, but of course there isn't one. And where would I write it anyway? On the cloth napkin? On my hand where Kyle would see it? This dress doesn't exactly cover a ton of skin.

I stare at her phone number, willing it into my memory. The area code is the same as everyone around here, so I recite the last seven digits to myself a few times. 927-3862. I want to run a search on her number when I get home, but that requires remembering it that long.

I glance around and get a jolt when I see Kyle headed back toward me. With a shaky hand, I place his phone back on the table, face down. I hope it's in the right spot. He sees me and smiles, holding up a saltshaker. I try to smile back.

927-3862.

He slides into his seat and sets the salt in front of me.

"Thank you," I manage. My heart is going crazy fast. He didn't notice anything, right? I salt my food the tiniest amount, even though it doesn't actually need it, and take a bite.

Kyle reaches for his phone and checks the screen, presumably for any missed calls or texts. He frowns. My stomach lurches. Did I close out of the emergency contact screen? But Kyle just sets the phone back on the table, face down again.

"Is that better?" he asks.

"Mmm. Yes," I take another bite. 927-3862.

I sip my water and dab at my mouth with my napkin, like I imagine a lady might do. I feel a little ridiculous. I hope I've done enough 'interrogating' and 'intel gathering' for today because I don't think my nerves can handle anymore.

"So, what do you like to do?" I ask. 927-3862. "For fun?" I can't quite bring myself to ask what fills his heart with joy.

He wipes his mouth with his napkin and takes a sip of water.

"I enjoy spending time exercising," he says. "I find it raises my endorphin levels and gives me a wonderful amount of energy."

"Oh, that sounds nice. What do you do for exercise?" I take a small bite of food, hoping that's okay to do in the middle of a conversation. 927-3862.

"My personal trainer has me working on increasing my endurance," he says.

Of course he has a personal trainer.

"Lately we've been focusing on running."

"That sounds delightful," I say. That's sounds awful, I think. 927-3862.

Kyle smiles, and his smile makes my brain stutter. Wait, was it 3862 or 2863? Uh oh.

If I was a painter, I would seriously want to paint his smiling face and maybe put it in a locket so I could look at it 24/7. Or make it into a huge portrait that I could hang above the fireplace and he could smile down at me for the rest of my life. I want to keep that smile forever.

He goes back to his food and my brain reboots.

3862. It was 3862. I'm pretty sure. 927-3862.

If I want him and his smile to stick around, I have to make sure he isn't the next victim on a crazy lady's hit list.

927-3862.

# Chapter Twenty

TURNS OUT LUNCH WITH Amanda isn't a, "Hey, let's meet up at a chic restaurant and order over-priced salad" kind of thing. It's a "Hey, let's meet up on my private yacht and have my personal chef cook us fresh seafood" kind of thing. These rich people. I'm having a hard time adjusting to their ways.

"Have a seat," Amanda says, gesturing to the cute white chairs around the small table on the yacht's deck. She settles back in one, crossing one long tan leg over the other. "We'll be setting sail in just a moment."

Layla and Lola aren't here, which gives me a moment of pause. I don't know if I've ever seen Amanda without her side-kicks. It's like my eyes need a moment to adjust to just one of her.

I smooth the front of my dress - the same one I wore to

the restaurant - and try to sit gracefully. Amanda probably suspects that this is the only nice dress I own, and I even considered buying another one, but my bank account couldn't take it. I just hope she doesn't comment on it.

The swaying of the boat is making me a little nauseated. The view would probably be beautiful if the sun weren't so blindingly bright on the water. I wish I'd brought sunglasses. Amanda has a large white pair obscuring her eyes behind rose tinted lenses.

"I'm so glad you could come!" she says, both her smile and her voice bright in a way I've only heard her use with her friends before. It gives me a strange sense of vertigo, hearing her talk that way to me.

I wonder, not for the first time, why I agreed to this. Mostly I was just curious why Amanda would want to have lunch with me, of all people. I figured it would give me something to laugh about with Fred later. But if I'm completely honest, part of me has always wanted to be seen by people like Amanda as a competent capable person. An equal. Now that I'm here though, with Amanda smiling at me instead of looking down her nose, I feel distinctly uncomfortable.

She leans forward and pours tea into two china tea cups. I feel like I should be on a southern porch, not on a lake.

"Do you want cream and sugar?"

I nod. "Yes, please."

She uses silver tongs to drop a sugar cube into my tea cup

and then pours cream from a smaller pitcher before handing me the cup and saucer. "It's mint tea," she tells me.

I nod and take it, sipping at it but it's too hot to really drink yet, so I set it on the table in front of me. The wind whips at my dress, whooshing the skirt up to expose my thighs. Blushing, I clap my hands down on the skirt and try to tuck it under the sides of my legs. Thankfully Amanda didn't seem to notice. She's placing a single sugar cube in her tea, tight-fitting dress unruffled by the wind, hair pinned up, ankles crossed.

I suddenly realize why I feel so uncomfortable. I'm a fraud. Amanda might think I'm on her level now because I'm dating someone rich and handsome, but it's a lie. A big fat lie.

The queasy feeling in my stomach deepens. I really hope Amanda doesn't realize how much of a fraud I am during this luncheon. But more importantly, I hope Kyle never notices. I want to belong in this world. I want to be capable and immaculate and poised.

I sit up straighter.

"So," says Amanda, setting down the pitcher after pouring cream into her own tea. "How long have you and Kyle been dating?" Her grin is mischievous.

I try not to fidget. I wish I had sunglasses for multiple reasons now. They could hide my nervous eyes. "Since Valentine's Day," I say, which isn't a lie. Not really. Right?

"That's so exciting!" she says, and she sounds like she means it. "I had no idea. You simply have to tell me all about him!" She reaches over and swats my leg as she says this, like we're old chums.

I flinch at the touch and clear my throat. "He's nice." That's it? "Um. Like really nice. And sweet. He bought me these earrings."

"Aww, that's adorable!" says Amanda. "Isn't it nice to have someone in your life that just worships the ground you walk on?"

"Yes. Yes, it is." Worship the ground I walk on? That seems a bit of an exaggeration. But I latch onto this possible topic shift. "How are you and…" I struggle to remember Amanda's fiance's name, but she jumps right in.

"Oh, Todd is a darling! He just showers me in presents! He is so sweet! He actually got me this yacht."

"Oh, wow! That's nice of him." A whole yacht? Good grief!

But then again, Kyle bought Jillian an apartment.

"What else has your Kyle bought for you?"

I frown at this uncomfortable question, like we are going to compare gifts and see which boyfriend is better. But right then the chef arrives.

"Ladies!" he says, throwing out his arms as if to embrace us both. He's short and muscled, with darker skin and black hair slicked back into a ponytail. I would guess he's of Asian descent. The mustache and little goatee are actually working for him. His eyes crinkle with the hugeness of his smile. "It is my pleasure to get to cook for you today! And who is this,

Lady Amanda?"

Lady Amanda? I try not to snort.

"This is my good friend, Amy-Kate," she says.

Since when are we good friends? I guess since I started dating someone worth her notice.

"Lady Amy-Kate!" the chef says, and this time he really does embrace me, which catches me off guard. But unlike Amanda, who's affection is calculated, this man seems genuine and positively overflowing with happiness. I find myself laughing a little as he lets go.

"I am so glad to have you here today!" he says. "I will make the most amazing food for you! You will never forget this meal!"

"Awesome!" I say, grinning. Then realize that probably isn't a word refined rich people use.

But the chef is grinning even broader now if that is possible. "Yes! It is awesome, isn't it?"

Amanda clears her throat, bringing the attention back to her. "Amy-Kate, this is Hinata. He's one of the best seafood chefs in the country."

"No, no, please," he says, waving his hands. "The praise is too much. I am just a man who likes food. And, thankfully, the food likes me too!" He is still grinning.

His happiness is infectious, and I realize I might actually enjoy this luncheon.

"Now, please," he says. "Tell me what you ladies want to

eat? Anything in the wide ocean and Hinata will get it for you!" He gestures at the lake as he says this, like we're actually sailing out at sea.

"I'll have lobster tail," says Amanda. "You know how I like it."

"That I do, Lady Amanda!" says Hinata. "One perfect lobster tail coming right up! And for you, Lady Amy-Kate?"

Maybe the title doesn't sound half bad after all. "What are my options?"

"Anything!" he says. "All the options! The ocean is my kitchen!"

I swallow. "I'm, uh, not actually very familiar with seafood," I say, clenching my folded hands in my lap and, of course, blushing.

Amanda makes a "tch" noise under her breath.

The illusion is already falling apart. "Could you give me a few choices?"

To my surprise, Hinata's smile grows even bigger. "You are new to this kind of food?"

I nod. "I mean, I've tried a few things, like shrimp, but I haven't loved it." If gagging counts as not loving it. "So I could use some recommendations."

"Oh, Lady Amy-Kate," he says, putting his hand to his heart. "It is an honor to cook for you today. I will make you the best food you have ever eaten in your life. Your whole life! Okay?"

"Uh, okay."

"It will be a surprise," he says. "The best surprise you ever had!"

I raise my eyebrows. "Oh, okay." My nervousness level goes up a few notches. What if I hate this guy's food? He seems so happy to be cooking for me and what if gag on what he makes me? I swallow and vow to do my best to not gag.

Hinata bows. "Ladies," he says. "Enjoy your sunshine and your time with a friend. I will return with the best food you have ever eaten." And he leaves, whistling to himself.

# Chapter Twenty-One

"HE ISN'T EXAGGERATING," says Amanda. "He really does make the best food in the world."

I nod. "I believe it." If you like seafood.

Silence descends in Hinata's absence and I take a sip of my tea, which has cooled to an acceptable temperature, just for something to do. As I set the cup down, the boat rocks and the cup misses the saucer, catching the edge of the tiny plate and tipping over, sloshing tea all over the table.

My face goes beet red. "Sorry!" I say, reaching for my cloth napkin and soaking up the tea.

When I manage to look at Amanda, she is still smiling, though it looks slightly forced. "Don't worry about it," she says. "Hinata can take it away when he comes back."

I nod and inhale slow and steady through my nostrils,

trying to cool my face. My stomach is roiling. I put a hand to it, trying to calm my nerves.

"So," I say, trying to take the focus off me. "How do you know Kyle?"

Amanda gives a small laugh. "Oh, Amy-Kate. You have such a sense of humor!" She pushes me playfully on the shoulder. "What I want to know is how you two met."

This is safe territory. I can talk about this. "It was actually at a little coffee shop, Beans and Bakes. Do you know it?"

"I can't say that I do," she says, eyebrows raised. "But I will have to visit sometime."

I smile. "It's very..." What's a word Kyle would use? "... quaint? I like the atmosphere. Anyway, we started talking while we were waiting for our hot chocolates, and he asked me out."

A faint line appears between her eyebrows. "Just like that?"

I shrug, smiling. "Just like that."

"Hmm." She looks like she doubts my story.

I go to take a sip of my tea again, not wanting to mention why he asked me out, only to remember I spilled it all. Amanda doesn't offer me more, and I feel too self-conscious to help myself to her tea.

"Where is the coffee shop?" she says, pulling out her phone. "I want to look it up."

I give her the cross streets and she types them into her

phone, nails clicking on the screen. Why do some girls like wearing long nails? It is a mystery I have never understood. They seem like more of a hindrance than they're worth. And they don't look pretty, at least in my opinion. They look more lethal than anything, like wild animal claws. Then again, maybe that's why they wear them.

She pulls up the place on her phone. "Oh, it looks so sweet," she says, scrolling through the pictures available. "I'm so glad you told me about this place. I simply have to go and experience it for myself. I love finding little places like this. They're so chic."

"Oh," I say. Chic. That would have been a good word. "I hope you like it." The thought of Amanda being in my little coffee shop gives me a little shudder. That is my place. My safe haven. I don't want Amanda telling all her cronies about it and invading it. But I guess it's too late for that.

"I can't believe I didn't notice it before," she says. "I've been to that section of town a few times looking at a building for rent out there. But-" She waves her hand, airily, "it wasn't big enough for what we need. You see, we're looking to expand the Finsetti makeup line locally, but when your business is as big as mine is, you simply can't settle for just any old place to set up shop."

I nod. "I see. I didn't know there was an empty building right around there."

Amanda nods. "Well, you would know if you had a business like mine. I simply have to be in the know about these sorts of things."

I think of mom's flower shop. We'd thought about expanding, a long time ago, but decided against it.

"What exactly is it you do for work again?" Amanda asks.

I cough. "Oh, uh. I work for Isomo."

"Oh, that's right! But that wasn't how you met Kyle?"

She knows where he works? That kind of gives me the creeps. How exactly does she know him? I don't think I can handle finding out she's another ex of his.

"It's a big company," I say.

"Yes, yes it is," she says and smirks.

I get the distinct impression there is something to this conversation that I am not understanding.

Just then my phone chimes. "Oh, sorry!" I say, pulling it out to silence it. It's a text from Fred.

Fred: How is the mission going?

"Oh my goodness!" Amanda says, leaning forward and reaching for my phone. "What an adorable phone case!"

I swipe to clear Fred's text from the screen, not wanting her to ask about him. Then I blink. "Wait, my phone case?" I've had this case for years. The flower design is faded on the plastic, completely rubbed away in places. I guess it was cute back in the day, but it is well past it's time.

"Can I see it?" Amanda asks, taking the phone out of my hand before I can answer. "This is so vintage!" she gushes.

"Where did you get it?"

"Uh." Vintage? That's a nice way of putting it. "I don't remember."

"Well it is incredibly cute," she says, running her fingers over it. "I've been looking for a case just like this."

"Oh." I take a sip of tea so I don't snort with laughter. I guess if you start dating a handsome guy and wearing nice dresses - well, one nice dress - people assume everything you own is suddenly expensive and "chic."

"Anyway," I say, taking my phone back from Amanda. I try not to clutch my stomach which is definitely feeling unwell. I need something to take my mind off it. And decide to do some reconnaissance - step three - just like Fred was asking about. Amanda seems like a well-connected person. "Do you know a woman named Jillian? Jillian Lynch?"

My search on Jillian's phone number last night brought up nothing. It was disconcerting. I even searched my own phone number to see what sorts of things it should bring up and was disturbed to learn that my name, address, and even past speeding tickets were available for anyone willing to cough up a few bucks. But not Jillian's. There was no address listed. No name even. Just, "Unknown."

Amanda purses her lips. "Can't say that I do." She sips her tea. "Why do you ask?"

I try to think of way to talk about her without it sounding like I'm jealous of Kyle's ex. Because I'm totally not. He's with me now anyway. Sort of. "She's Kyle's ex," I say, waving my hand like Amanda did a moment before, like it's nothing.

Amanda's eyes narrow. "His ex is still hanging around him?"

I shrug. "It's no big deal. I was just curious if you knew her."

"Wait, did they break up recently?" Amanda asks.

"Uh, yes?" I realize I don't actually know how recently they broke up.

Amanda nods. "I've heard about her! She gave the paparazzi a headache trying to get a decent photo of her. That woman knows how to dodge a camera." She sounds impressed.

"Oh?" I say, like I didn't spend a whole day stalking her online and come to the same conclusion. "Wait, the paparazzi?" Why were the paparazzi trying to get a photo of her?

Amanda nods enthusiastically. "No one really knows anything about her. Strange woman. I'm amazed you've actually met her! I figure she must be someone rich and famous, not wanting the attention like that. Poor people always love being in the spotlight."

I swallow, still trying to calm my stomach. "Mmm. So you don't know anything about her? Like, where she's from or anything?"

Amanda shakes her head. "No one does. She's this mystery woman! Quite fascinating."

This was useless. At both getting information and distracting me from my nausea. "Could I get more tea?" Mint soothes your stomach, right?

"Of course," says Amanda, gesturing to the tea pot. "Help yourself." She goes back to her phone.

I stand, then wobble as the yacht sways underneath me. My stomach heaves. I place my hand over my mouth and reach for the tea, desperate to calm my stomach. The boat lurches and I stumble, crashing into the table and upsetting the pitcher of tea just as my stomach heaves again. And this time, everything comes out. I retch, vomit spewing from me like a cartoon, straight onto Amanda's form fitting dress.

# Chapter Twenty-Two

FRED BURSTS OUT laughing. "Seriously? You threw up on Amanda's dress? I would have loved to see her face!"

"Shhh!" I scowl and shift, trying to find a position where branches aren't poking every one of my body parts, but give up. Hiding in the bushes at sundown is way overrated. But I guess this is what I get for agreeing to go along with step four - spying. "You're not supposed to laugh! It was terrible! I've never felt so humiliated!"

Fred keeps laughing, but at a much quieter volume. "You're going to think it's hilarious in a few weeks," he says. "Trust me."

I roll my eyes. "Anyway, we need to focus."

"How are you even still alive?" Fred asks, clearly not ready to let it go. "I would have expected her to murder you!"

"She was weirdly calm about it, actually," I say. I guess whatever prompted her to invite me to lunch and be nice to me dictated she not get upset about me vomiting on her dress too. "Like, it was kind of freaky how robotic-ly calm she was. And anyway, she doesn't matter! She's not the one we're investigating. Could you please focus?"

"Maybe you gave her a mental break down."

"Fred!"

"All right, all right. I'm focusing." He puts his eyes back to the binoculars, but gives another chuckle. "Why did she invite you to lunch anyway?"

I haven't told him about the dates with Kyle. I know I should, but for some reason I don't want to. So I shrug. "I told you. I ran into her and she invited me."

"Yeah, but, why? Like, really, what possessed her?"

I rack my brain for a way to change the subject, and peer through the bushes. "Maybe she had a change of heart?"

Fred snorts.

This feels like a stake-out, like we're FBI agents or something. It also feels pretty boring. And poky.

"Anyway, she didn't know anything about Jillian. She said that no one knows anything about her. She a mystery woman."

Fred nods and reaches across me to grab his backpack and yank it through the branches toward him. I've very aware of his nearness.

"Granola bar?" he asks, thankfully dropping the Amanda questions.

I shake my head, too nervous to eat. "I should never have let you talk me into this. We're going to get shot!"

Fred raises an eyebrow. "You underestimate my stealth abilities. Besides, how else are we going to get enough information to take to the police? Steps one through three were a bust."

Fred shoves the backpack behind him. The bushes are so loud! Every twitch I make rustles them and snaps twigs.

"We'd better hope she doesn't have a thing against squirrels or stray cats," I say. "Because it sounds like there is a whole herd of them in these bushes!"

"A herd of squirrel cats?"

"You know what I mean!"

"Shhh!" Fred ducks down further in the bushes, binoculars pressed to his eyes.

I freeze, sure Jillian-the-serial-killer is coming to investigate the racket in her bushes. Nothing happens for an agonizingly long time. My breathing is so loud.

"What was it?" I breathe.

"Never mind." Fred lowers the binoculars. "It's some other lady just walking her dog. I thought it was her. They both have blond hair."

"Ugh. Give me those. I'll recognize her."

Fred hands them over and adjusts his position.

"What exactly are we hoping to see anyway?"

Fred shrugs. "Evidence. We won't know it until we see it. Maybe she'll get in a car and we'll take down the license plate number and find out it was at the scene of the crime or is a stolen car. Maybe we'll overhear a private conversation about something illegal she's done."

"She's not going to have a conversation like that outside."

"Maybe-" Fred says with a mischievous glint, "we'll see her burying a body!"

I shiver. "Whatever. That is super unlikely. Unless it's us she's burying."

I put the binoculars to my eyes and peer through the bushes. It's dark and hard to see and the foliage isn't helping anything. "Are you sure this is the right place?"

"Yep," says Fred. "You said she lives next door to Kyle, and that's his place right there."

I don't know if I'm more worried about being seen by Kyle or Jillian. "He said he bought her the apartment next door. These are not apartments."

"I guess when you're a billionaire anything that isn't a mansion is an apartment."

Seriously though, this place is way nice. It's like town homes for millionaires or something. The row houses are huge with immaculate front lawns and trimmed hedges, which we are currently trying to hide in. The place is even gated. We had to wait until someone entered and sneak in behind their car.

"Wait!" I clutch Fred's arm. "That's her! She just left!"

"Are you sure?" He leans forward.

"Shhh!" I track her as she walks down the sidewalk, looks left and right, and then ducks behind her building. That was definitely sketchy behavior.

I stand, showering leaves. "We have to follow her!"

We dart out of the bushes, Fred grabbing his backpack and tripping over the branches, and make it to the corner. Standing to the side, I peek around then motion for Fred to follow me. My heart is pounding. I feel like I'm some secret agent in a movie.

Is it bad of me to hope that I'm right? That Jillian really is the serial killer and we'll catch her doing something incriminating and then Kyle won't be able to get back together with her because she'll be in jail?

We scurry after Jillian as she treks across the neighborhood and to the gate that encloses it. She punches in a code on the front gate for the community, and exits. We pound toward it, but it slides closed behind her, blocking our way.

# Chapter Twenty-Three

"WHAT DO WE DO?" I ask as we run up to the gate, now closed.

"Climb," says Fred. "We can't lose her!"

Fred cups his hands to give me a boost up and I raise my eyebrows. "Seriously?"

He grins. "You've got this."

Gritting my teeth, I grasp the bars of the gate and step into Fred's hands. He hoists me up so easily and quickly my leg almost buckles. He really isn't that scrawny kid from high school anymore. I swing my free leg over the top of the gate, which is thankfully flat.

"You good?" Fred asks.

"Uh, sure." I am not good. The gate didn't seem this high from the ground. Am I supposed to jump down?

Fred hoists himself up next to me like he does this every day. He seems to sense my hesitation as I sit there, straddling the gate and eying the ground. "I'll jump down, and then help you," he says.

I nod.

He's down in one lithe movement and reaching back up for me. He's tall, but so is the gate, and his hands only reach my calve. I swing my second leg over.

"Jump," he says. "I'll catch you."

So I close my eyes and let myself slip down off the edge.

Fred, true to his word, catches me under the arms and slows the last of my fall, setting my feet gently on the ground. He grins at me.

His smile is so close, so genuine, that my heart gives a lurch.

"Come on!" he says before I have time to even register the strange feeling. He grabs my hand and pulls me after Jillian.

We peer around the corner and into the next street. Jillian is making good time in those heels. She's way down the street and when she turns a corner, we have to scramble to follow. Neither of us has any practice following someone, and I'm not sure how far back we need to stay. Her apartment was in the nice part of town, but the further we go, the less nice things get. The streets get narrower and the buildings get distinctly unfriendly looking until I start to worry more about getting mugged by a stranger than getting caught by Jillian.

Fred puts his arm protectively around me as we pass a group of men smoking on a street corner, but they don't seem interested in us. A couple of them stare after Jillian, though. Still, Fred's arm around my shoulders is nice. If I was by myself, I would have turned back a while ago. This is not a place for a young lady to be walking around at night.

At last, after what feels like about an hour of walking, Jillian stops in front of a shop. She starts to turn, and we duck into the nearest door to hide, finding ourselves in an antique shop. The old man behind the counter looks us up and down as he blows out a stream of smoke from his cigar.

"Can I help you?" he asks.

Fred moves in front of me. "I think we have the wrong place. Sorry, sir." He pushes me back out the door. Jillian is gone.

We walk to the shop Jillian stopped in front of and carefully look in one of the windows. It's a pawn shop. Places like this always give me the creeps. But this one looks especially seedy. There are gaudy jewelry pieces in the window with what has to be fake jewels because I don't think real gems even come in those sizes. A gold watch glitters on a faded purple cushion. Jillian is standing at the counter inside, with her back to us. A man at the counter appears to be arguing with her.

We watch as we walk slowly past, not wanting to dawdle and draw attention. I can't see what they're arguing over though. Is Jillian pawning something? That doesn't make a lot of sense though since Kyle is paying for practically her whole life still. Why would she need more money?

"Do you think she's buying something?" Fred asks.

"Maybe."

We pause on the other side of the shop, just out of view.

"Now what do we do?" I ask.

Just then, the door to the pawn shop opens. In one swift move, Fred puts his arm around my waist, and spins me around, holding me close to him, his back to Jillian.

I catch my breath. I don't think I've ever been this close to Fred before, my stomach pressed against his. I can smell his scent - not heady cologne like Kyle wears but just a distinct masculine smell that is somehow even better. I swallow and focus on his tshirt. I can just see the top of an atom.

I peek over his shoulder and see Jillian walking away. She doesn't seem to have recognized me. That's a relief. So why is my heart still racing?

Fred's Adam's apple bobs as he swallows. He doesn't let go of me, so I raise my eyes to meet his. Were his hazel eyes always this gold? How did I not notice before?

He bites his lower lip, making me glance at his lips. My face instantly heats. Am I thinking about kissing him? Good heavens! This is Fred! Just Fred! My best friend. My hilarious, confidant, good-looking best friend…

Oh no.

I suck in my breath and drop my gaze. Fred loosens his

arm around my waist and I step away, face still burning. Stupid blush.

"So, uh." I cross my arms and look around. "We should probably keep following her, yeah?"

"Yeah," Fred says, his voice a little breathless. "Sure. Good idea."

Without looking at each other, we start jogging after Jillian.

"Thanks for hiding me," I say. "That was quick thinking."

"Of course. No problem," he says.

We turn the corner and then have to scramble to back track. Jillian is standing in the alley. And she's holding a gun.

# Chapter Twenty-Four

I dial the non-emergency police number again with shaking hands. Is this an emergency? Should I have called 911? But no one is dead or dying. Yet.

"Police station. How can I direct your call?" a male voice asks. This feels weirdly deja vu.

"Uh, I called earlier? About a woman?" Why do I sound like I am asking a question? "I have more information on her."

"Do you know who you spoke to before?" the man says.

"Um, no."

"Okay, one moment."

A woman's voice comes on the line. "This is Officer Rhodes. What can I do for you?" It's the same officer! I am sure of it.

My hand is sweating. I don't know why I'm so nervous.

I'm not the serial killer! But what if she doesn't believe me again?

"I called earlier," I say, clutching the phone to my ear. "About a woman. Her name is Jillian Lynch and we just saw her buy a gun."

There's a beat of silence. "Buying a gun is not illegal, ma'am." Officer Rhodes sounds impatient.

"I know! I know it's not. I'm pro-gun rights and all that. It was just in this really sketchy part of town and I don't think she has a license."

The woman sighs. "I'll make a note. Thank you for your concern. Have a good day."

"Wait!" She still isn't taking me seriously. I have to convince her to look into Jillian, not just make her useless notes! "I really think she might be the serial killer," I say. "Like I said before. The one from the news. There are no pictures of the serial killer, and there are no pictures of Jillian, like anywhere. And there isn't any information listed online about her. Can you like, run a background check or something at least?"

The officer sighs again, like she is trying to have patience. "Just because a woman is private and doesn't post her whole life story on the internet doesn't mean she is a criminal, ma'am. Have a good day." The line goes dead.

"Well?" Fred asks as I lower the phone from my ear.

I shake my head. "No luck. She just sounded annoyed."

Fred frowns. "The whole point of our list was to get information for the police!"

"If the police aren't concerned," I say, "then maybe I just need to drop it." Maybe I'm wrong. Maybe she isn't dangerous.

"Yeah, she's just crazy and has a gun," says Fred. "That's all."

Yeah. That's all. And my gut says that Kyle is in danger, even if the police don't believe me.

# Chapter Twenty-Five

I PULL INTO THE small airport, not sure what to expect. Kyle called to ask if I could meet him here. He said he had something to ask me. Which sent my heart into palpitations.

Are we going to be official? Does he want me to be his girlfriend?

I park my car and look around. In the distance, a helicopter is grounded and spinning it's propellers, throwing wind around that I can feel even all the way over here. Other than that, it seems pretty deserted. Thank goodness it's daytime or I might be concerned that serial-killer-Jillian got ahold of Kyle's phone and lured me out here. I shiver.

I need to tell Kyle what Fred and I saw. My cheeks flush. I push the thought of Fred firmly out of my mind and focus instead on Kyle. I want to date Kyle. And I need to talk to Kyle.

I need to keep him safe because he is almost definitely being stalked by a serial killer.

And then I catch sight of Kyle.

He's across the airfield, small but distinct in his blue suit coat that is flapping in the helicopter wind. I swallow at the sight of it. The nerves I felt about talking to him double at the sight of him. I unbuckle my seatbelt, then take a few deep breaths. I'm already blushing. I press the backs of my hands to my cheeks, trying to cool them, but one more look at Kyle undoes it all. This blushing thing really is a curse. I hope he thinks it's cute. He's never commented on it. I spit out my mint gum into the wrapper and check my breath. Minty fresh. Perfect for kissing. I apply another layer of lip gloss and rub my lips together, smacking them in the rear-view mirror.

Taking a deep breath, I clutch my purse to my chest and open the car door. I am about to be Kyle's girlfriend. I am beautiful, and Kyle likes me, and I am going to be his girlfriend.

I tug at the hem of my skirt. This is the same nice dress I wore to our last date. The only one I own. But I'm hoping Kyle is the type of guy who doesn't notice outfits too closely.

I look great, I tell myself. I can totally pull this off. I wobble in the heels and catch myself. Thankfully, Kyle hasn't noticed me yet. He's looking to the side, talking to another guy, and he looks like someone in a model photo shoot with artificial wind. He is so perfect, so poised, so immaculate. Even the wind looks like it was made to accentuate his features, tousling his hair. The feeling of self-consciousness deepens, like he's some immortal god and I am a lowly commoner playing dress up.

I take another deep breath. He likes me, I tell myself. He thinks I am pretty. He's going to ask me to be his girlfriend. I think.

I hope.

He looks over and sees me, waves and heads toward me. I smile back and start to hurry toward him, but another wobble on my heels slows me down. The last thing I need is to embarrass myself falling literally head over heels in front of him. Or is it heels over head? As I get closer, I almost have to lean into the wind to get through it. It doesn't make walking in these ridiculous heels any easier. And even worse, I have to slap my hands down over my skirt to keep it from blowing up and showing off my undies to the world. I wish they would turn the helicopter off.

"Amy-Kate!" Kyle calls when we're close enough to hear each other. He has to shout to be heard. "I'm so glad you made it!" He reaches me and takes my arm, which I appreciate for multiple reasons. His hand is warm and firm and I feel a little less like I might blow away. He turns and leads me straight for the helicopter.

"What are we doing here?" I ask.

He points to the helicopter. "I want to take you on a ride."

My eyes widen for half a second before the wind stings them and I squint again. I'm sure I look a fright, tottering in my high heels, eyes squinting like a little old lady, and my hair whipping around like a horse's tail swatting flies, and getting stuck in my lip gloss. Lovely.

We reach the helicopter and I gulp.

"I've never ridden in one of these," I shout, in case that isn't obvious.

"That's all right." He helps me inside.

"And I'm afraid of heights!"

He smiles as he climbs in next to me. "I'll keep you safe."

Well, all right then. I picture his arms around me as we fly. Maybe this won't be so bad after all.

But no. We get buckled into separate seat belts, so I guess him holding me isn't going to happen. But at least we're side by side.

"How are you today?" Kyle asks. We still have to shout even with the helicopter door closed, trapping us in this metal monster.

"Oh, uh..." I try to think of something fancy and wonderful to say, like he always does. "I'm... uh. Top of the morning!" I wince. He's not British! "I'm good. Yeah, I'm good."

His smile deepens. "I'm glad to hear it."

"Where are we going?"

He just smiles. "It's a surprise."

My stomach tightens. I hope I like this surprise.

We don't talk much as we fly. I don't really want to shout over the noise about him being stalked by a serial killer. Hopefully we're going someplace quieter. Instead of talking, I focus on not being motion sick. I hope my face isn't green. At least that would be a change from the usual red.

Finally we touch down and I want to thank whatever gods there are in the universe for getting me safely back to solid ground. Kyle unbuckles me and I don't even think about his hands brushing my collarbone as he undoes the clasps. Well, okay, maybe I think about it a little, but mostly I think about getting off that flying machine.

If people were meant to fly, we would have been born with wings. I like the ground, thank you very much.

I stumble out of the helicopter and almost face plant in my heels, but Kyle is fast enough to catch me. He pulls me against his chest as I get my balance back, and then fight back the nausea. I take deep breaths of his cologne and fresh air as the helicopter powers down. The silence it leaves behind is ringing. Only when the wind and nausea subside do I realize how close we are. My hands are against his chest, his arms around me. My breath hitches, my face heats. I peek up at him and see him looking down at me, smiling that soft melting smile.

"Thank you for coming," he says.

"Of course! I'm always happy to go places with you."

"I'm glad to hear it."

His eyes are such a warm brown, with the setting sun hitting them and tinting them gold. I could look into them forever. I want to look into them forever.

"Amy-Kate," he says, his voice breathless. "You look beautiful tonight."

I instantly turn scarlet with pleasure and look away. "Thank you." I seriously hope he thinks the blush is attractive, or the whole looking beautiful thing just went out the window.

One of his hands lets go of me to touch my cheek, bringing my gaze back to meet his. I feel shy now, looking into those eyes, but try to hold my gaze steady. His thumb caresses my cheek.

"I have something I want to ask you," he says, his voice low.

"Yes?" I'm breathless.

His hand cups the back of my neck, gently, and his thumb touches the place below my earlobe. I remember him putting in the lily earrings for me. This is more intimate. More heart-stuttering. More everything. Just more.

He leans in.

This is it, I think. He's going to kiss me. He's really going to kiss me! I seriously hope he likes the taste of mint gum! I wonder what he'll taste like.

I close my eyes, trying to stop my crazy thoughts, wanting to savor the moment, wanting it to never end.

"Will you," Kyle whispers, his breath against my lips, "be my girlfriend, Amy-Kate?"

# Chapter Twenty-Six

MY HEART THRILLS. I feel drunk with him so close. "Mmm-hmm," I say. "Yes." Just kiss me already!

His lips meet mine and they are soft and warm, His hand at the back of my neck pulls me to him like we aren't close enough.

But my brain doesn't shut off. Instead, what I think is, "What if Fred saw me right now?"

My stomach twists and I squeeze my eyes shut and kiss Kyle harder, trying to make my brain shut up. I don't care what Fred would think. Kyle is the one I want to date. Kyle is amazingly attractive and poised and perfect. Kyle is the man of my dreams. Kyle.

Kyle pulls away enough to break the connection and smiles at me in a sleepy way, like he's drunk on our kiss.

I tuck my head against his chest and he puts his chin on my head.

I am Kyle's girlfriend, I think. That is wonderful. Amazing.

Why do I feel sick? Probably just left over nausea from the helicopter ride.

And then I realize what I am looking at. I'd been so caught up in Kyle I didn't realize where we were.

"Holy cow!" I say, snapping my head up and thwacking my head on Kyle's chin. "Ow! Sorry!"

I rub my head and he touches his chin, but doesn't look annoyed.

"Where are we? Paradise?"

He chuckles. "Welcome to my private island, Amy-Kate."

We are on a white sand beach with palm trees and, in the distance, a huge white mansion with glittering glass windows. I feel like I just stepped into a Hollywood movie.

"Your private island? Seriously? Where are we even?"

Kyle slides out his phone. "I'll show you." He pulls up a digital map and leans over so that our shoulders are touching, showing me his phone screen. I can feel his warmth through his jacket.

He zooms in on the huge lake I went sailing on with Amanda the other day. I never realized how huge the lake is. When he's so zoomed in all I can see on the screen is blue, he points at the middle of the screen. "Right about there."

I squint. "I don't see an island."

He chuckles. "I paid to have it taken off most maps. You'll be hard pressed to find anyone who knows about it."

Frowning, I point out the obvious. "But don't boaters come across it all the time? Surely you can see it from the water."

He tucks his phone away, shaking his head. "There are shallows around the island for quite a ways preventing boats from coming close. That's why we flew in on helicopter."

Smiling, he reaches out and takes my hand and I get a thrill of pleasure at the touch.

See, I tell myself. That thrill proves it. I totally like Kyle. Only Kyle.

And I'm holding hands with my boyfriend! Squee!

I'm such a dork.

"Let me show you around," he says. "I know it's a little cold out here, but the beach house has a fireplace and there should be hot cocoa waiting for us."

Did he just call that mansion a beach house?

"Is it peppermint hot chocolate?" I ask.

"What else would it be!" Hand-in-hand, he leads me up the beach.

As I try to walk through sand in heels, I think of Jillian. Has she been to this private island? I know I finished all the steps on our list of how to save Kyle, but we still haven't saved him, and I'm not giving up.

When we get inside, he helps me out of my coat. My stomach is in knots, trying to think of how to start up a conversation about his serial killer ex-fiance. I shiver.

"Come and sit by the fire," he says. "It will drive away the chill."

I nod and follow him into a large living space with a soft white rug and low white couches with gold throw pillows. A fire blazes in the hearth, and I think it's an actual fire, not just an electric one. Sure enough, there are two mugs of steaming hot chocolate on a coffee table along with a plate of tiny cookies. I can smell the peppermint as I sit down on one of the couches.

Kyle sits beside me and slides his arm around me like it's the most natural thing in the world. My heart jumps at the touch. I swallow and reach for my hot chocolate.

"So, I've been thinking," I say, not sure how to make this conversation happen besides just plowing ahead with it.

"Mmm?" Kyle asks, reaching for his own mug.

"About Jillian."

Kyle frowns and turns to look at me, taking his arm from behind me. "About Jillian?"

I nod.

"I told you, you don't need to worry about her," Kyle says. "Things are over between us."

"I know," I say. "It's not that. I was just watching the news and I have some suspicions."

Kyle's frown deepens. He sets his mug back on the coffee table, untouched. "Are you talking about the story on the news involving a murderer and several millionaires?"

I nod and watch his reaction, wondering if he'll believe me.

Kyle shakes his head. "I told you, Jillian is hardly the type to commit murder."

"I know you think that, but no one expects someone they know to turn out to be a murderer! And she seems really suspicious!"

Kyle leans back and crosses his arms. "What has she done that is suspicious?"

I swallow and collect my thoughts, wanting to present them in a logical way that he'll understand. "The serial killer always gets engaged to a rich man and gets written into his will and his life insurance. Then she kills him and takes the money. Jillian became your fiance, got written into your will, and then was super upset when you broke things off with her."

"It's understandable for her to be upset," Kyle says. "Anyone would be upset after a break up."

"True, but what about your will?"

"I think it's natural to want to be assured that you will be taken care of by your life partner, should that person have an unfortunate accident. I don't think there is anything wrong with being written into your future spouse's will or life insurance policy."

"Okay, but what about taking pictures? There are no pictures of this serial killer fiance and Jillian has no pictures of herself anywhere. She's not on social media! I mean, have you ever seen a picture of her?"

Kyle shakes his head. "Social media has many flaws, which Jillian doesn't appreciate. Honestly, I think it's a healthy practice to limit time spent on social media."

I grit my teeth. "Do you know that she has a gun?"

He raises his eyebrows. "Yes, and owning a gun isn't illegal. Many people, especially women, own guns simply for personal protection."

"Yes, but-" I let out a frustrated noise. "Look, any one of these things by itself wouldn't be suspicious, but when you add them all together, you have to admit there is something weird going on here."

Kyle is studying me with a look of concern. I'm coming to hate that look.

"Amy-Kate," he says gently, putting his hand on my arm.

I stiffen at the condescension in his voice.

"I know you aren't happy that I dated Jillian, but don't you think this jealousy is clouding your judgment of her?"

I glare at my hot chocolate in my hands. "I just wanted to warn you," I say. "You should be careful around her. That's all. I don't want you to get hurt."

Kyle takes his hand away and nods. "Thank you for your concern."

His words remind me of the officer's and I scowl as I take a gulp of hot chocolate.

# Chapter Twenty-Seven

FOR SOME REASON the idea of Kyle in our little house above the flower shop makes me feel uncomfortable. I stand in front of my grandmother's mirror in my same nice dress I've worn several times now. He's bound to notice that I only ever wear one outfit around him at some point. I wonder if I could return this dress, get my money back, and buy a different one.

I slip on some pink heels and look around the place, seeing it the way I imagine Kyle will see it. It's so small with one poky hallway leading from the front door to the cramped living room smushed up against the kitchen. Everything is older than I am and very out of date. I never realized how badly this place needs a make over. Things that once seemed familiar and cozy now seem dated. The carpet is brown shag, threadbare in places. I remember dragging my stocking feet over it as a kid, making my hair stand up with static electricity. Couldn't we have replaced it sometime in the past few decades? There are pictures of me as an awkward teenager on the walls that I seriously want to hide or burn. The whole place reeks of sentimentality.

I just keep thinking of Kyle's mansion on his private island. But, I have to remind myself, that wasn't where he grew up. Probably.

I wouldn't have invited him over here except that Mom insisted. She said it was ridiculous not to invite my boyfriend to my birthday party.

"It's not a party," I said. "It's just us."

"All the more reason to invite him."

She had a point. I can't hide my life from him forever. I might frequent the same "chic" little coffee shop that he does, but our lives are nothing alike. I can only hope he finds this place charming and cozy instead of ugly and embarrassing.

The knock on the door sounds and I bolt forward to look through the peephole. Not Kyle.

"Rachelle!" I throw open the door. "I didn't know you were coming!"

She grins and hugs me. "Your mom invited me. And look-" she holds out her empty arms. "Baby free too! Scott's watching her for the whole afternoon, bless him! I am so ready for this party!"

I can't stop smiling as she comes in and I close the door. "I feel like I haven't seen you in forever!"

"I know, right?" She takes in my dress. "Oh, wow!" she says, looking me up and down. "That dress is gorgeous!"

"Yeah?"

"Uh, yeah. I don't think I've ever seen you this dressed up before. This boyfriend must be someone special!"

I nod. "Yeah."

"Oh, here! Happy birthday!" She produces a small present from her purse.

"Can I open it right now?"

She laughs. "Of course! That's what birthdays are for!"

I rip off the yellow wrapping paper to find a lemon scented candle. I open it and smell it. "Oh my goodness! This is divine! I want to eat it!"

She laughs. "I'm glad you like it!"

"Did you make it?" She runs a business from home making things like lip balm, lotion, and candles. All of them smell heavenly.

"Of course!"

The doorbell rings and I jump.

Rachelle's grin gets bigger. "Is that him?"

I shove the candle onto the nearest shelf and smooth down my dress. "How do I look?"

"Amazing."

Just be normal, I tell myself as I walk past her and take a

deep breath. He likes me. It doesn't matter what my childhood house looks like. He likes me.

I open the door. "Hey, Kyle!"

He smiles. "Amy-Kate, you look magnificent!" He's holding a small present wrapped in silver paper with a little pink bow atop it. "Happy birthday!"

"You know you didn't have to," I say, cheeks pink, as I take the gift.

He leans forward and for a moment I think he's going to kiss me, right in front of Rachelle. My heart practically jumps out of my chest. But he only pecks his lips to my forehead.

"For you, on your birthday, I would buy you anything," he whispers.

"Come in," I say, to hide my blush. Though, logically, I realize that if he was going to be dissuaded by my blushing, it would have happened a long time ago. "This is Rachelle," I say, standing between them. "Rachelle, this is Kyle."

"Nice to meet you." Rachelle shakes Kyle's offered hand.

"The pleasure is all mine, I assure you."

Rachelle raises her eyebrows.

"My mom made cake," I blurt out. "It's just the four of us. Not much of a party, really, but my mom's baking is always delicious! I mean- she's not a world class chef or anything, but-"

"That sounds wonderful," Kyle smiles warmly. "I love homemade cake."

I let out a breath. "Oh good."

They both follow me down the poky hallway while I silently plead for Kyle not to notice the awkward photos of me on the walls. If he does, he doesn't comment. And then through the cramped living room - navigating around the couch - to get to the kitchen.

"Was Amanda not able to make it?" Kyle asks.

I tense.

"I know you two are good friends. I assumed she would be here as well."

"Amanda?" Rachelle asks, snorting. "Like, Amanda Finsetti?"

"Uh, oh look, we're here!" I gesture to the kitchen.

Mom is wearing an apron, flour on her cheek, hair in a messy bun. I cringe. Couldn't she have cleaned up a little for this? She's washing dishes, the sink full of soap suds, rubber gloves on her hands.

"Kyle, this is my mom. Mom, Kyle."

"Oh, yes. We've met," Mom says looking over her shoulder at him. "Hello, Kyle. Hello, Rachelle."

"Hey, Mrs. Hillsdale," says Rachelle.

"Good evening, ma'am," says Kyle. "Thank you for inviting me into your home."

Mom waves this away, soapy water flicking off her fingertips. "Sit down. Make yourselves comfortable. The cake will be out of the oven any minute now."

I give Kyle a tight smile and gesture to the table that I spent twenty minutes clearing before he arrived.

"Thank you," he says, and takes a seat. He looks a little stiff, like he isn't sure how to act in this new environment. I don't blame him. I feel the same way. Rachelle slides into a chair on the opposite side of the table. Weirdly, she looks uncomfortable too.

I want to go hide in a hole. Why is this so awkward?

The doorbell rings.

I frown and look at Mom. "Did you invite someone else?"

She shakes her head. "Might just be a package delivery."

"Be right back," I say and go to answer the door.

When I look through the peep-hole, my heart gives an unexplained leap. It's Fred.

# Chapter Twenty-Eight

I GLANCE BACK down the hallway to make sure Kyle didn't follow me, and then answer the door.

"Hey," I say, slipping out and closing the door behind me.

"Happy birthday!" Fred says, beaming and holding out a gift. Then his gaze takes in my dress. His eyes widen. "Oh. Wow." His cheeks go a little pink. I tuck some hair behind my ear self-consciously. I don't think I've shown this much skin in front of Fred since we were kids in our bathing suits.

He swallows. "You look really nice," he says, gesturing to the dress. "I mean, you always look nice. No matter what you wear. I've just never seen you in a dress like that before. It's almost like a different you."

"Is that a good thing?"

He shrugs. "I mean, if you like it, then yeah."

I shift in the dress and heels. Do I like it? "Honestly, it's kind of uncomfortable," I admit.

He clears his throat. "Well, happy birthday!" He gives me the wrapped present.

"Thank you!" I take it, almost hesitantly. It's light and a little floppy. The wrapping paper crinkling as it moves.

"You thought I forgot, didn't you?" Fred asks.

I laugh. "No. You never forget!"

He grins. "Open it!"

I do, peeling back the paper to reveal a white t-shirt. I unfold it, letting the wrapping paper fall to the ground. On the front of the t-shirt is a picture of three roses, all perfect and glossy, and next to the roses is a sprig of Queen-Anne's lace. Underneath in cursive it says "Be your own kind of beautiful," except the word "beautiful" is in a different font, all crazy and the letters different sizes. For some reason, I feel like I might cry.

"Hey, you okay?" Fred asks.

"I love it," I whisper. "I just, really love it."

"I'm glad."

I swallow and fold the t-shirt up. "Thank you."

"Of course!"

I lean down to gather the discarded tissue paper and Fred gets down to help.

"Hey," he says. "I was wondering- Would you like to go on a date with me?"

My heart jumps out of my chest. I swear I can feel it flopping around like a fish on the ground in front of me. My gaze snaps to him.

He's looking at me in a way I've never seen before. Is he... shy?

His eyes are hazel, which I knew, but I guess I haven't really looked at them recently. Because right now they seem foreign. I realize he's dressed nice, in a blue plaid button up and his wild hair has been combed. He looks nice. Really nice. When did he get so... grown up? He's not a teenager anymore. Not by a long shot.

My breath catches.

"I hope it doesn't make things weird, me asking you out," he says. "I just- I want to give us a chance, you know. If you want. Because, I like you, Amy-Kate. I like you a lot." He sucks in his breath.

I can't breathe.

He takes the rest of the crumpled wrapping paper from my hands, and our fingers touch. I feel it, but I don't pull away. We're crouched there, eye to eye.

The tears are very close to coming now. Why? Why do I feel like crying? This is ridiculous. This is just Fred. Awkward, silly Fred. Just my best friend. Just the guy who is hilarious and who I feel totally comfortable around. The guy who was there during my awkward years and who is very much not awkward anymore.

"Hey," he says, reaching out and putting a hand on my cheek, brushing away a tear. "It's okay. Don't be sad! If you don't want to go on a date, it's okay. I promise I'll still be your friend and we can forget any of this ever happened! I just figured I should tell you before I explode because I think you are so beautiful and so funny and so smart and so kind. And I just- I would really love to go on a date with you."

I sniff. And then the door opens behind me.

"Amy-Kate?" It's Kyle.

I jump away from Fred like he burned me, scrambling to my feet, which is not easy in heels, and wobbling a little.

Fred and Kyle both reach out to steady me, one hand on each arm, and I see their eyes meet.

My cheeks heat up and I step back, away from them both.

"Are you all right?" Kyle asks. "I got worried when you didn't return. I thought someone might have kidnapped my girlfriend!"

I wince as Fred takes a step back, looking like he's been slapped.

"I should go inside," I say. "I'm feeling a little dizzy." I feel like one of those Victorian ladies in a corset, saying I need to lie down for a moment. I should get some smelling salts.

"Let me help you," Kyle says, putting his arm around me, like he's marking his territory. He kisses my hair as he leads me inside, and I get the distinct impression he does it specifically for Fred's benefit.

"Thank you for the present," I say over my shoulder to Fred as Kyle leads me inside. "I really appreciate it."

Fred just stands there, looking lost, until Kyle closes the door in his face.

Later, when I open Kyle's present, I find two red rose earring studs, all glossy and clearly expensive.

"They're beautiful," is all I say.

# Chapter Twenty-Nine

I STARTLE AWAKE to the sound of the Star Wars theme playing.

"What the-" I look around wildly, trying to find the storm troopers that are invading my room, until I see my phone lit up. I grab it. Fred is calling. And then I remember that he changed his ring tone while I was at his house playing board games last time. He had said it would be a surprise. He was very right.

"Hullo?" I say.

"Have you seen the news?"

"Uh." I scratch my head and swing my feet onto the floor. "What time is it? Isn't it Sunday? Why are you awake this early?"

"Have. You. Seen. The news." Fred sounds a little annoyed.

I guess he hasn't forgiven me for having a boyfriend I didn't tell him about. But I'm the one who got woken up practically at light saber point.

"You know I don't watch the news," I say, but I'm padding into the living room anyway.

"Well, you should turn it on. Channel 23."

I sigh. "Okay, okay. But if it's something depressing, I'm going back to bed. Wait, channel 23? Isn't that like a gossip thing? Amanda was talking about it. It's like rich people talking about celebrities and stuff. Why are you watching that?"

"Do you have it on yet?"

"No. Sheesh! Give me a minute. I'm trying to get my brain to boot up." I give up on finding the remote and press the power button on the TV, then flip though channels manually.

"Are you sitting down?" Fred says. "You might want to be sitting down."

The tone of his voice gives me a chill. "I'm flipping channels," I say. "Give me a minute."

Channel 23 comes to life and my hand freezes. There, filling up my entire 48" TV screen is a photo of me and Kyle.

Me! And Kyle!

"What the-" I sink back on the floor, not bothering to back up to the couch. The photo is of us outside the King's Restaurant. On the other end of the line, Fred doesn't answer, but voices on the TV are talking.

"-an unknown girl. This is the first time Kyle Kincade has been seen in public with another woman since the Jillian Lynch fiasco."

My eyes are almost popping out of my head. "What the-" I say again, this time a whisper.

The image cuts to two women in glittery dresses sitting in comfy arm chairs with a small table between them. "You know," says one of them with a blond bob, "You have to admire how quickly he picks girls up. It was right before Valentine's Day that he and Jillian ended things in that messy break up."

The other woman, older with skin that looks plastic, like it's been injected a few too many times with anti-wrinkle serum, nods. "That was a messy break up indeed. Ms. Lynch has declined our invitations to appear on the show, but maybe this new mystery woman would be willing to come in and give us some of the details about her and her new lover." She grins.

I feel myself blushing. Lover? We just barely became exclusive! And what do these women care anyway?

"Now, we don't know who this woman is, but we do know she has a great fashion sense," the blond woman says.

"Oh my, yes!" the older woman says. "Just look at that dress. The image of perfection. Though, the woman herself could stand to lose a few pounds!"

The two of them chuckle.

I flush deeper.

"Anyway," says Fred loudly through the phone. I jump, having forgotten he was there. I am a statue, my arm frozen with the phone to my ear. My eyes glued to the TV screen as they say, "Her make up is lacking as well. With small eyes like that, she really needs to make them pop, you know what I mean? But, as we've seen in the past, Kyle Kincade doesn't always go for the classic beauties."

I feel sick.

"Amy-Kate?" Fred says. "Are you still there?"

I don't answer. I can't.

The women on the TV are laughing. Another picture fills the screen. Kyle and I leaving the restaurant. It's a terrible shot. My hair is blowing over my face and I'm caught mid-sentence, my mouth open and my eyes half-closed mid-blink. I look like an idiot.

"Her haircut leaves much to be desired as well," the older woman's voice says over the image. "It looks as if she hasn't been to the salon in ages!" They both laugh.

The picture of us is replaced by a photo of just Kyle. A posed photo that was obviously professionally taken. Kyle has one hand on his lapel and is looking straight into the camera.

"Kyle Kincade's taste in woman has varied over the years," The blond woman says. "It's always exciting to see who he'll bring home next! As the youngest CEO of his time, Kyle Kincade has made Isomo the leading tech company in the United States, but he's much more well-known for his steamy love life! Who is this mystery woman and what is it about her that attracted the attention of the most eligible bachelor in the country?"

The image dissolves and the two women smile. "Up next, dresses that have taken the runway by storm!"

It cuts to a commercial and whatever force was holding me in place snaps. I collapse onto my back, staring up at the ceiling as a jingle for hair shampoo plays on the TV.

"Amy-Kate," Fred says softly. "I'm sorry. I didn't know they would say those things. I should have thought of that. I'm so sorry."

"Why were you watching that?" My voice is hollow. "Why were you watching old ladies gossip about people they don't even know?"

"I wasn't. I mean, I only turned it on when I heard-"

"Who did you hear from?"

"It was on social media. Amanda posted on the high school page saying you were on TV."

I feel like I'm going to puke. "Is he really the CEO of Isomo?"

"You didn't know?"

I close my eyes and press my palm to my forehead. "How would I have known? You know I don't like keeping up with the news! Especially not celebrities!"

Fred doesn't answer. "Are you really dating him?"

I feel like I am going to cry. I take a deep breath. "Yes."

Fred exhales. "And he didn't tell you?"

I rub my forehead. I'm an idiot. "He said he worked for Isomo."

"Maybe he thought you already knew. I mean, most people recognize him."

I think of Amanda saying I was so funny when I asked how she knew Kyle. She recognized him. Probably everyone recognizes him when we go out together. It wasn't his bearing or his fancy suits that people respected. They reason they looked at me like they did was because they knew he was the CEO of Isomo. I'm such an idiot.

"I have to go," I say.

"Are you okay?"

I give a laugh. More of an exhale than anything humorous. "No. I don't know. I just really have to go." I hang up.

A second later my phone rings. I think it's Fred again for half a second, but it's not the Star Wars theme playing. My heart lurches thinking it's Kyle. But no. It's Rachelle.

I pick up.

"Are you okay?" she asks. "I just saw the news! I'm coming over!"

I burst into tears. Best friends are awesome.

# Chapter Thirty

AN HOUR LATER, I've eaten half a gallon of chocolate ice cream, ignored five calls and seven texts from Kyle, and ranted until I've run out of steam.

"At least it's something good," I say, lying on my bed, looking over at Rachelle. "The secret he was keeping."

"True." Rachelle spins in my desk chair, catching herself with a bare foot on the side of my desk. "But it was still a lie."

"Not really." I push myself up on my elbow. Now that I've calmed down and had my tirade, things aren't seeming as bad as I thought at first. "He told me he worked for Isomo."

Rachelle snorts. "He doesn't work for Isomo. Isomo works for him."

I flop back down. "Same difference."

Rachelle raises her eyebrows but doesn't comment.

"I've missed this," I say. "Hanging out with you. Talking on the phone just isn't the same."

"I know." Her face is wistful. Then the baby starts crying in her pack and play in the living room. Rachelle checks the time on her phone as she stand up. "A whole hour? Wow! That was a miracle of a nap if there ever was one!"

I swing my legs off the edge of the bed and follow her into the living room, watching as she lifts the crying baby and holds her close.

"And this is why we don't hang out much," Rachelle says. "I don't want you to lose your hearing before your time."

I laugh. "Whatever. She's one of the most well-behaved babies I've ever seen!"

"Then you haven't seen her on her bad days." Rachelle shifts the baby so she can look at her, and smiles. "You can be one tough cookie, can't you," she says in a baby voice, cooing at the girl. "Can't you?"

The baby gives a smile and makes some sort of noise I couldn't imitate if I tried. I grin. "She's adorable. You have to give her that."

Rachelle smiles. "So, are you ready to call him?"

I sigh and then square my shoulders, and nod.

"Good luck," says Rachelle. "We'll be out here if you need some baby therapy after."

"Thanks."

Back in my room, I shut the door and lean against it, taking a deep breath. Then I call.

He picks up on the first ring. "Amy-Kate?"

"Hey," I say weakly.

"Oh, thank goodness. I've been trying to get in touch with you. Are you all right?" The concern in his voice softens my hard edges, just a little, and I sink onto the floor.

"Yeah," I say, rubbing my forehead. "I think I'm all right."

The insipid voices of the women on TV come back to me. "...could stand to lose a few pounds... ...not a classic beauty..." I shut my eyes, trying to block them out.

"So you saw?" he asks.

"I saw." My voice is hollow.

He doesn't say anything.

"Why didn't you tell me?" I ask.

"I am so sorry," he says. "I wanted to. I really wanted to."

"Then why didn't you?"

He sighs. "Can we meet in person to discuss this? I feel this is a conversation that should happen in person."

I debate. Do I want to see him right now? If I'm totally honest, not really. But I should give him a chance to explain.

"Fine," I say. "Meet at your place in thirty?" For some reason I don't want him at my place right now, and knowing who he is, I don't want to meet in public either.

He hesitates. "I actually have a meeting in just a few minutes that I can't back out of. How about in an hour?"

Seriously? He can't cancel a meeting for me? But I guess

he is a big shot. And I had no idea.

"Fine, whatever," I say, and hang up.

The silence left behind is broken by happy baby giggles from the next room. I open the bedroom door and lean against the door frame.

"That was fast!" Rachelle is sitting on a blanket on the floor, bouncing Fiona who is squealing in delight.

"He wants to meet in person to talk about it."

"Uh-oh."

"What?"

Rachelle shrugs. "I think he just wants to win you back into his good graces with his handsome face."

I blush.

"Did he at least say he was sorry?"

I nod.

"Well, that's something. Call me after if you need me. Promise?"

I smile. "Promise."

Rachelle nods, satisfied, and stands up with Fiona. "You know," she says, "Fred seemed really concerned when he called me."

I blush. Stupid Hillsdale curse. "Yeah?"

"Yeah."

# Chapter Thirty-One

I DECIDE TO HEAD OVER to Kyle's early. I know he won't be home from his meeting for another forty-five minutes, but I want time to collect myself. I want to be able to look at his home and process the fact that it belongs to a famous billionaire before I have to look at his face and process that belonging to a billionaire too.

I punch in the code for his gated community, understanding now why he needs privacy like this. Otherwise the news and paparazzi could camp out on his lawn whenever something interesting happened.

Wait, are they going to camp out on my lawn now? Not that I have a lawn, living in a second-story apartment, but are they going to swarm me as soon as my identity gets out. I cringe. I seriously hope not.

The gate slides open and I drive in, painfully aware that my old car does not fit in here. Thankfully the streets are empty and quiet. I pull up in front of Kyle's "apartment" and cut the engine, looking around. Maybe I'll go for a walk. The landscaping is beautiful and the sidewalks are shaded by big old trees.

I get out and lock the car, but Kyle's apartment window catches my attention. I wonder why for a moment, and then see it again. Movement. It's the first story window. His curtains are open, but his front lawn is big and I'm too far away to see much. Frowning, I walk closer. Surely no one could have broken in. He's got to have a great security system. Maybe he has a maid?

I walk across the lawn and up to the window, just to make sure no one is robbing him.

Peering in the window, my heart stops. It's Jillian!

I duck under the window and out of sight. What is she doing alone in his apartment? Poisoning his food? Setting some deadly trap? I knew she was up to no good!

Crawling closer to the window, and into the flower bed - sorry daffodils and tulips! - I lift my head just enough to see inside. There's Jillian. She's just standing there, arms folded. In profile to me. Is she debating the best way to commit her murder?

And then Kyle walks into view.

My cheeks color, but not with embarrassment. This time,

it's with anger. He said he had a meeting! Guess I found out who this oh-so-important meeting is with!

He's holding two drinks and hands one to Jillian who takes it with a frown.

I suddenly realize my position, crouched in someone's flower bed, peeping in their window, in full view of the neighbors. Anyone in their right mind who sees me will call the cops. I need to get back to my car. Walk away. I don't need this. If Kyle is going to lie to me and meet with his ex when he's supposedly dating me, and prioritize spending time with her instead of apologizing to me, then he isn't worth my time. I am so done with him.

Then I pause. But what if Jillian really is going to murder him. Just because he's a jerk doesn't mean he should die. And if I suspect he's in danger and do nothing, does that make me complicit?

I sigh. I don't need this. I glance in the window.

And see Jillian, turned away from Kyle, reach into her purse and pull out her gun.

I gasp and spring to my feet. I don't think. I just move. I launch myself at the window, banging on it with both fists.

Both Kyle and Jillian jump and turn to look at me.

"She has a gun!" I scream, still banging. I point furiously at Jillian. "A gun!"

Kyle gives Jillian a bewildered glance, oblivious to the danger he is in, and turns his back on Jillian to leave the room. My heart is racing so fast I feel light-headed. Jillian is still holding the gun, and when she turns toward me, I duck to the right of the window, out of sight, aware that she could probably shoot me through the glass.

A moment later, Kyle comes stomping around the side of the house.

"Amy-Kate? What are you doing here?" He doesn't sound happy.

I point at the window. "She has a gun! She was about to shoot you!"

He stares at me like I've lost my mind for a moment.

"You need to call the police right now! She's dangerous!"

Kyle closes his eyes and rubs his forehead. "Amy-Kate." His voice is serious and low. "This obsession is ridiculous."

"I'm serious! She-"

"She was returning my gun!" Kyle says, his tone angrier than I've ever heard it. "I lent it to her a few months ago because she didn't feel safe at night. And now she was giving it back!"

"What? No, I saw her buy the gun at this sketchy-"

Kyle shakes his head and lets out a hard breath of air. "This is unbelievable. How long have you been spying on her?"

"I wasn't spying!" Well, right now anyway.

"You just happened to be in a 'sketchy' part of town and saw Jillian picking up my gun from the repair shop?"

I swallow. Repair shop? Have I been wrong about this whole thing?

# Chapter Thirty-Two

I SHAKE MY HEAD and gesture to the window. "I just saw movement and thought someone might have broken in."

"And that's why you showed up an hour earlier than we had arranged?" Kyle asks.

"Maybe if you weren't lying to me and having secret meetings with you 'ex' we wouldn't be having this problem!" My anger builds. "Plus, we shouldn't have had to have this meeting in the first place! Because you shouldn't have kept a secret like who you actually are from me! Especially if you knew that people might take photos of me and talk about me on TV!"

Kyle deflates a little. "I'm sorry. I said it on the phone, and I'll say it again. I'm sorry. I know I should have told you. I was just being selfish. I liked how you saw me - as a regular person. It was refreshing. I thought your perception of me would change if I told you. Everyone I've dated has always seemed more interested in my money and status than in me. You're different. You saw me, the real me. I guess I didn't want to lose that. I'm sorry."

I bite my lip. Maybe I hadn't known he was a famous CEO, but I had noticed how much money he had. And I liked it. I liked it a lot. Did I like it more than I liked him? Would I still like him if he were broke?

I shake my head. Of course I would! I'm not a shallow gold digger!

"I should have told you," Kyle says. "It wasn't fair, keeping it from you."

I nod. "You should have told me."

"I'm sorry," he says again. "But there's no harm done. I think we should put this behind us and move forward. Together." He reaches for my hands.

I jerk them away. "No harm done?"

He looks a little taken aback. "They don't even know your identity. It was just a couple of photos and some gossip. Things like this happen all the time."

I blink in surprise. "A little bit of gossip? Did you hear what they were saying about me on TV?" Not a classic beauty. Could stand to lose a few pounds. Their words pound through my head like a drum beat. "Do you think I'm okay with people talking about me like that for everyone to hear? They might not know who I am now, but plenty of people who do know me saw that broadcast! How long do you think it will take for them to figure out who I am?"

Kyle looks distinctly uncomfortable. "It really isn't as big of a deal as you think it is," he says. "They say things like that about people all the time. Besides, if you are going to date me you'll just have to get used to it. There's no sense making this into a big deal."

"The reason it's a big deal," I say, struggling to keep my voice calm, "is because you didn't give me a choice. I didn't choose this. Maybe I would have, but now we'll never know because you didn't give me that option. If I'd gone into this relationship knowing all the risks and then this happened, that would be one thing. But you never told me!" I jab my finger at him.

His eyes narrow.

"And Jillian!" I say, gesturing at the house. "With all the secrets you've been keeping I wouldn't be surprised if you knew all along that she's a serial killer and have been covering for her!"

Kyle shakes his head like he is deeply disappointed in me. "Not this again. I explained to you, Amy-Kate, that she is not a murderer."

"And how would you know that?" I spit out. "She's after you, Kyle. And I'm done trying to warn you and protect you! You can just take care of yourself from now on because-"

"She's leaving," Kyle says.

"What?"

"Jillian's leaving. She got a job across the country, terminated her lease, and moved out of her apartment. She's getting on a plane in an hour."

This throws me. "Are you sure? Maybe she's just pretending to leave so you'll let your guard down-"

"I'm sure! Would you stop with this nonsense? Her apartment is empty! Someone else already signed a lease for it and is moving in next week. It might have taken a while for the reality of our breakup to sink in, but now that she's accepted it, she's moving on with her life. She isn't after my money. She isn't trying to kill me! So stop with all of this talk about my ex-fiance being a criminal!"

I swallow, cheeks burning. If she really is moving across the country, it can't be her. Can it? Maybe she saw it was futile and moved onto her next target?

Kyle groans and rubs his temples. "Look, Amy-Kate, can we please get this conversation back on track. I'm sorry I didn't tell you everything about my life when we first met. I've apologized, okay. Let's move past this."

I frown and look up at him. "I can't just move past this. It's a really big deal to me! You kept multiple secrets from me, and I didn't keep any from you!"

"None?" Kyle asks, one eyebrow raised.

Something about his tone gives me pause. "No, none!"

"You were upset when you found out I was helping Jillian

with her finances, but you were going on dates with another man!"

"What? Wait, Fred?" I ask. "We're best friends and I wasn't going on dates!" I really hope my flaming cheeks aren't getting any redder. Now is not the time to be thinking of Fred. I keep my eyes firmly on Kyle's. This is between me and Kyle. And I need to stay focused.

"We hung out as friends - just friends!" I struggle to keep my blush under control. "And that was before we were even official!" I gesture between us. "I wasn't dating anyone until a week ago!"

"I wasn't dating Jillian either," Kyle says. "I told you we broke off our engagement. I just met with her over dinner to help her with her finances." He sounds like he's accusing me of something.

"Okay! Fine!"

"So I wasn't cheating on you!"

"I didn't say you were cheating on me!" I said you were being stalked by a serial killer!

"Well, good," he says.

"Good."

The silence sits between us, heavy and suffocating.

"Look." He straightens his suit coat, hands on his lapels. "I don't want to date someone who doesn't trust me."

I clench my fists into my pants. It feels like the ground might be sinking under my feet and I want something solid to hold onto.

Kyle isn't looking at me. "I didn't think you were going to be the jealous type."

I swallow. I'm not jealous! I'm angry that my boyfriend doesn't believe me and that he kept secrets from me! Am I being un-reasonable?

"Maybe this isn't going to work out like I hoped," says Kyle.

The sinking sensation deepens, pulling me downward.

"What are you saying?"

"Maybe it's best if we don't see each other anymore." He looks away.

My chest is tightening. I can't breathe well. "Fine," I manage. "Fine."

The silence is suffocating. I clench my purse strap in my hand and look away. Jillian is standing at the window, frowning at the two of us. Can she hear us through the glass?

I turn and walk away, in stupid heels that poke little holes in the grass and make me stumble. Catching my balance, I straighten my shoulders and march to my car, feeling ill and humiliated.

If we were going to break up, why did it have to be in front of Jillian, of all people.

Worst. Day. Ever.

# Chapter Thirty-Three

INSIDE, I KICK OFF my shoes and squirm around, trying to unzip that awful dress. I finally manage to peel it off and then crawl into a baggy sweater and jeans and wrap myself up in a blanket. I don't cry.

I feel so stupid.

Shortest relationship ever.

There was this one fling I had the first summer of college that lasted just a month. I figured that would be my shortest relationship. I was wrong.

The pain is dulling in the quiet and for some reason, that makes me mad. I want to feel the pain of this moment. I want it to hurt. I want to cry. Maybe I just want to get it all over and done with, feel it all and let it all out at once instead of suffering though this ache for days on end.

I grab the TV remote and turn it on, flipping to the gossip channel Fred told me to watch this morning. But it's a different program now about celebrities' dogs. Kyle doesn't have a dog. Not one that I know about anyway. Judging from the number of secrets he's withheld from me though he could be a dog trainer for the circus and I wouldn't be surprised. I flip channels, trying to find something about Kyle, something to spark the pain, something to make me feel. Sadistic, I know.

But there's nothing on about Kyle at the moment. Not a single program. So I settle for watching the next best thing - the depressing news. They're still going on about the dead millionaires killed by that crazy fiance.

Perfect. Another thing to remind me of my failures in life. I huddle down in my blanket and prepare to be depressed.

The detective himself comes on screen. "Again," he says. "This is the first and only picture we have been able to find of the fiance."

I sit up straighter. They found a picture?

The picture in question comes on screen. It's a grainy black and white, like it was taken from a security camera and zoomed in. "We suspect she used disguises," the detective says, "but we are hopeful that facial recognition software will be able to discover her true identity."

I squint at the photo. It's a woman all right, seen from behind, in a dress and head scarf, looking over her shoulder. Only a portion of her face is visible. I can't tell much from it, but she looks oddly familiar. I swear I've seen those eyes before. I shiver.

My phone rings and I jump. It's Fred. My heart gives a weird flutter as I answer.

"Amy-Kate."

"Hey, I'm not really in the mood for-"

"Turn on the news!" Fred cuts me off.

"What?"

"Turn on the news!"

"I'm already watching it!"

"Wait, really?" He sounds momentarily surprised. "Never mind. Are you seeing this?"

"What channel are you on?" I ask.

"The one about the murderer with the detective and the picture! Are you seeing this?"

"Uh, I see the picture. It's pretty blurry though."

"It's not Jillian," says Fred. "It's-"

"Wait, shhh!" I stand up, looking around. Did I just hear a click, like a lock turning?

"What is it?"

"Shh!" I strain my ears, listening. It was probably just my imagination. I'm feeling spooked because of the news is all.

"We were wrong," says Fred.

"I know! Be quiet a second!"

And then I hear the unmistakable sound of the door handle turning and the back door clicking open. My heart seizes in my chest. I duck down behind the kitchen island.

"Fred," I whisper. "Someone's here. In my house." My voice is strange and high. "I have to call the cops."

"In your house?" Fred asks. "But why would she-"

"I have to go." I hang up. My hands are shaking so much it's hard to hit the numbers.

9-2- I hit the delete button. 9-1-

A bag descends over my head and tightens around my neck. I lash out with my hands, hitting someone, but to no effect. Whoever it is keeps one hand on the back of the bag and grabs my wrist with the other, gripping so hard I drop the phone.

I inhale to scream, but it turns out that is exactly the wrong thing to do. I register a chemical smell and a burning at the back of my throat before everything goes dark.

# Chapter Thirty-Four

I COME TO WITH A splitting headache. In books and movies, people always have a blissful moment when they first wake up where they can't remember what just happened. I don't get that luxury. With the pain comes an acid hot fear in the pit of my stomach, clawing it's way up my throat. I might retch.

The cloth bag is still on my head. The smell is making me nauseated. I've heard you can kill people with chloroform-which is what I assume this is. Accidentally give them a little too much and wham. No waking up. I suspect that if that had happened, Jillian - who must be my kidnapper - wouldn't mind too much. I'm glad I'm still alive.

I shift, trying to locate my numb limbs. I'm lying on my side, hands tied behind my back.

"Oh, you're awake. Good."

I stiffen. That is not Jillian. I struggle to recognize the feminine.

"I need you to do a little favor for me."

Whoever she is, she sounds strangely detached from this situation as though she is talking about the weather a few states over.

"I'm sure you have a headache and you might vomit. That's all part of the side effects. Don't concern yourself about it too much. It will pass." High heels click on the floor as she comes toward me and I cringe away, accidentally hitting my head on a wall behind me.

She grabs the bag over my head and tugs it off. I blink at the brightness, gasping in lung-fulls of fresh clean air. Well, make that dank cold air. But I'll take anything over the chemical smell of the bag.

I look up. And then I gasp. It's definitely not Jillian.

It's Amanda.

Amanda Finsetti is crouched in front of me, head tipped to the side, assessing me.

I'm so shocked I just stare at her for a moment. She looks like she always does, minus her sidekicks. Her makeup is perfect. Her hair is immaculate. Her nails long as claws. And her ever-present frown is firmly in place. I am so confused. Is she working with Jillian?

I inhale and let out a scream at the top of my lungs,

screaming until my breath runs out. Amanda leans back a little. I take another breath and this time I scream words. "Help! Please help! I've been kidnapped! Help!" I end in a cough, my throat feeling raw from the chemicals.

"Are you finished?" Amanda sounds bored. "No one can hear you so all this screaming is pointless."

She stands and steps away from me, and I get a view of the room. It seems to be an unfinished basement with a cement floor and walls. A wooden desk is against the far wall next to a tall metal filing cabinet. There are no windows and just one door.

Amanda picks something up off the desk. A gun.

I freeze.

She levels the gun at me and my heart tries to jump up my throat.

"No more screaming," she says. "It's giving me a headache."

Then she picks up something else. My phone.

Amanda clicks back to me and I press myself into the wall, trying to get as far from her as I can. She crouches in front of me again and rests the barrel of the gun against my forehead.

I try to gulp but the saliva sticks in my throat. I can't breathe. This is it. The end.

"I need you to make a call for me," she says, holding out my phone.

I stare at her, not moving.

"Call Kyle Kincade, your cohort in all of this. Tell him to meet you here, now. Tell him it's urgent. The address is written down."

I see that there's a sticky note on my phone screen with an address printed on it in neat feminine handwriting. I recognize that handwriting from high school. This is Amanda, the hallway queen. My high school rival. This is Amanda. Holding me at gunpoint.

This cannot be happening.

"Take the phone," she says slowly. "And call Kyle. Or I will pull this trigger. And the world will be better off with one less fashion terrorist on the loose."

I stretch out my shaking hands, bound together at the wrists with a zip-tie, and grip the phone. The sticky note is hard to peel off. My hands are shaking so hard I almost drop the phone.

"Call Kyle," she says again. "And if you even think about trying to call for help instead, or telling him what is going on, you will be dead before the words leave your lips."

I don't doubt her.

I navigate to my contacts and call Kyle. I don't know if he'll even pick up, seeing as I'm now an ex-girlfriend. It rings. And rings. My hands are slippery with sweat. I don't know if I want him to pick up or not.

Then, "Hello?"

"Kyle?" My voice comes out hoarse and scratchy. I cough.

The gun digs into my forehead.

"What is it?" Kyle sounds mad.

"I- I need you to meet me. Right now. It's an - an emergency." I wonder if he can hear the terror in my voice.

"What's going on?" he asks, the anger giving way to confusion, and maybe even a touch of concern. "Are you alright?"

Amanda jabs a long nail at the sticky note and I cringe away from her.

"The address," I say, my voice still strained and raw. I have to shift my hands and head a little to read the sticky note with my hands tied together. "The address is 1986 Wainscott Way." I manage to swallow. "Please hurry."

Amanda snatches the phone from me and the gun finally leaves my head. The sticky note flutters to the floor. I stare at it. I'm shaking.

"This," says Amanda, "is why you shouldn't meddle in things that are none of your business."

# Chapter Thirty-Five

AMANDA COMES TOWARD me with a roll of duct tape in her hand. I jerk my head away.

She sighs, like I am a petulant child. Then she grabs a fistful of my hair and yanks it toward her so hard my eyes water. She kneels on my hair, pinning my head in place. She does all this with the same expression she had in high school when she would corner me in the hallway and make fun of my clothes, like I am something unpleasant she must suffer through. She pulls a length of tape away from the roll and rips it off.

I scream and try to bite her, but she calmly sticks the tape to one of my cheeks, waits for me to gasp for breath and claps it over my mouth, sticking it to my other cheek as well.

"You thought you were so clever," she says as she smooths the tape across my mouth making sure it's good and stuck, "you and Kyle figuring out who the killer is." She adds another piece of tape for good measure and then stands.

Me and Kyle? I have no idea what she is talking about.

I pull my head away as soon as my hair is free of her knee. I really hope I don't throw up with my mouth taped closed.

She crosses her arms and looks down on me. "How long have you been following me?" she asks. "I thought I was the one gathering intel on Kyle when I invited you to my yacht. He was my next target, but of course you already know that. But you wanted to be invited over, didn't you. The whole time, you were gathering intel on me! I should have seen it sooner. I thought it was just a coincidence - you showing up at that restaurant the same time as me. But you planned it didn't you. I have to admit, I didn't think you had it in you, Amy-Kate. Good thing I bugged your phone or you might have gotten away with all this."

I stare. Does she seriously think I was on to her?

"But I heard you on the phone with someone - it was Kyle, wasn't it? You were talking about how you figured out who the killer was. And that was your mistake."

It wasn't Kyle I had been on the phone with. It was Fred. She must have only been able to hear my side of the conversation if she thought I was talking to Kyle. And she bugged my phone? I remember her exclaiming over my "vintage" phone case and feel sick. I threw up last time we were together and I just might be about to throw up again.

"I don't know what Kyle Kincade sees in you," she says as she goes to the door. "You're not pretty or even very smart. But it doesn't matter because in an hour or so, this will all be over and neither of you will be around to bother me anymore. I won't get Kyle's money like I was hoping, but there are always other rich men waiting to be conned." She gives me one last look, then opens the door, flicks off the lights and goes out. I hear a lock click. And then another. And then a third.

Three locks? Seriously?

I lie still for a few minutes, as her heels click-click-click away, listening hard, trying to quiet the rushing in my ears. I don't know what I'm listening for exactly. Information I guess. I can use all the information I can get. Once her footsteps fade, I can't hear anything else. Just silence.

I stare into the blank darkness. Amanda? It was Amanda this whole time? How did I not see this?

My breathing is hard and fast. What am I supposed to do now? There's no way I can get out of this mess!

I need help. Lots of help. But I don't have my phone.

I can't do this. I can't. I was so completely wrong about everything. No wonder everyone thought I was crazy and my suspicions were unfounded! I was so convinced Jillian was the killer I never even suspected the real murderer! I had lunch with Amanda, for goodness sake! And she asked about Kyle.

Kyle Kincade. My boyfriend. Who I didn't even recognize as the CEO of Isomo.

I'm such an idiot.

Hot tears form, making my eyes ache, but I don't try to stop them. If there was ever a time for crying, this is it. I'm kidnapped, being held who knows where in some musty basement, about to be framed for multiple murders, and don't have long to live. Plus I now have snot running down my face.

My brain is all too happy to go down this road with me, reminding me of every single failure since high school, flashing them through my mind like a tally. Kyle dumped me because I wasn't good enough for him. The police laughed at me while I accused an innocent woman. I let mom down by not accepting the flower shop. I have a dead-end minimum-salary job I hate. I dropped out of college. I failed my high school algebra class. Twice! And I couldn't even keep that dang goldfish alive as a kid!

I am such a failure!

I sob, tears and snot running sideways down my cheek. They pool on the ground around my face and make everything so much grosser and pathetic.

I think of all the other women I know who are so much more capable than I am. They wouldn't be sobbing. They would be getting themselves out of this situation. They would be handling things well. They probably wouldn't have even gotten into this situation in the first place because they would have realized who Amanda was sooner and called the cops on her!

I remember my mom standing up to Jillian in the flower shop, unafraid and fierce. I remember Rachelle and how she manages to take care of her baby and work from home doing what she loves. How her life is so put together and wonderful. And I think of me. Living alone in a cheap apartment. No boyfriend. No company. Not even a goldfish. Nothing.

I am not the right person to survive a kidnapping.

Weirdly, I think of Fred right then and the t-shirt he was wearing at the reunion. The one with the cat in the box and how he said the shirt glows in the dark, only the cat is dead in the dark.

I'm that cat right now, trapped in the dark, waiting for someone to open the box and tell me if I'll live or die.

My tears are running out. I sniffle and shift around, finding the wall behind me. I wriggle around and manage to prop myself up against the wall, leaning my head back, hands squashed behind me.

No one is coming, I think. No one else is going to get me out of this mess. It's up to me.

The thought is not comforting, but it is oddly strengthening. It's terrifying, but if I'm going to have any chance of surviving this, I'm going to have to save myself. I might fail. I might fail miserably. But I won't let myself die without trying to live.

I sniff and think of Mom again, facing down Jillian like a bear protecting her cub. I felt like a little trapped bird at the time. But I can't be that bird any longer. I swallow and look up at the ceiling. It's time to find my own wild animal side.

I guess that means I need a plan. Dang it.

# Chapter Thirty-Six

STEP ONE IS TO get myself untied. I remember this video Rachelle showed me in high school about how to get out of zip ties using shoelaces. I seriously hope it works. I fumble around for my shoelaces in the dark. I get one converse untied and try to remember the video and how this works. It's harder than I thought it would be trying to poke the end of the shoelace through the zip tie with my bound hands. I have to do finger acrobatics and I drop the shoelace several time. My hands are sweaty.

I hear a sound outside the door and freeze. What if Amanda hears me moving around and comes to check on me?

I can't think like that, I tell myself. Just focus on the shoelace.

I finally poke the end of the shoelace through the zip-tie, right beside my hands, and then use my teeth to pull it through. Success! So far.

Now to see if it actually works. I hold the loose end of the shoelace between my teeth, pull the shoelace tight and then start sawing the zip-tie against it, running my hands up and down and up and down, faster and faster, praying the Internet didn't lead me astray and that the zip tie breaks before the shoelace does.

After what feels like forever, there's a pop and my hands fly apart.

I laugh out loud, but it's muffled by the duct tape. Hands free now, I rip the tape off my mouth, wincing a little.

I release my breath and grin. I flex my fingers and rub my wrists and then get to work on the ziptie around my ankles with the shoelace. When it breaks, I marvel that it worked a second time. I guess Amanda didn't count on me having seen Internet videos on how to escape when kidnapped. Ha! Thank you Rachelle for that weird spy phase in high school!

With my feet free, I stretch my legs out, then retie my well-worn shoelace and stand up. Maybe a little too fast because I get dizzy and have to put my hand against the wall. Maybe the chloroform is still making me woozy. I take a deep breath and wait for the dizziness to pass before making my way around the room to the door, one hand on the wall to guide me. I flip on the light and take a look at the door.

It has a handle with a keyhole, but I have no idea how

to pick locks. Why didn't Rachelle and I watch videos about that? And from the sound of deadbolts when Amanda left, there must be two other locks on the other side of the door that I can't even see. This isn't good.

Maybe I can break down the door? I go to the desk, opening every drawer, looking for something heavy and solid, but there are just a bunch of papers. Useless.

Then, as I'm closing the top drawer, I see a photo of Kyle half tucked under a pad of paper. My heart gives the customary lurch at seeing his handsomeness. It's like a primal reaction. It doesn't matter how mad I am at him, or how broken up we are, or how kidnapped I am. He is hot! I shake my head. I am so silly.

Sliding the papers away, I find a whole folder of photos. The first shot is a candid one. Kyle is in profile, talking on the phone and doesn't appear to know his picture is being taken. I dig through the pictures. They're all of Kyle, wearing different clothes, in different places. All candid shots.

Then I freeze. I'm in one of these photos. It's taken from outside the coffee shop. Kyle and I are standing inside talking, seen through the window, his phone held out toward me. I know this moment. This is when we met. This is when he gave me his phone to put in my number.

I shiver. I already knew Amanda was creepy. But having someone spy on me with a telephoto lens while getting hot chocolate? Ugh.

None of these photos are going to help me escape though, so I drop the folder back into the drawer and go to the filing cabinet. I try the first drawer. Locked. The second drawer too. They're all locked.

I go back to the desk and start opening drawers again. There, at the back of the top drawer, is a little silver key. I run to the door. It can't be this easy, I think, heart pounding. But maybe she forgot she had a spare key in her desk. She probably never planned on me getting out of those zip ties. Just maybe. If luck is on my side.

Luck is not on my side.

The key doesn't fit. At all.

Which now that I take more than half a second to look at it, should have been obvious. It's not a door key. It's too small.

I turn around and lean on the door, staring at the desk and… the filing cabinet!

The key fits perfectly in the filing cabinet's lock. I turn it and open the first drawer. It's filled with hanging folders. The name Benjamin Johnson is written on the first one. I frown. The name sounds familiar. I rummage further, just looking for anything escape worthy, but finding nothing. I close the drawer and move onto the second.

It's just more of the same, only this file says Dominic Rusher. I pause. This name is also familiar. I pull out a piece of paper at random. It's a floor plan of a house. I slide it back in and pull out another one. This is an itinerary labeled Average

Wednesday at the top. I run my gaze down it. It looks like an average Wednesday alright. Breakfast, commuting to work, working, lunch break, commuting home, stopping at a coffee shop to grab a donut. Each one has times and addresses written next to them. The paper is typed and printed, but written in cursive next to the lunch break is "egg salad sandwich."

With a start, I realize why I know these names. They're the dead guys from the news. These are two of the five rich men the detective thought were all the work of one crazy serial killer. I'm holding proof in my hands. My hand starts shaking and I slide the paper back into the filing cabinet.

I open the next drawer, knowing what I am going to find. And sure enough. There is another one of the victims - Liam Alvarez. I don't even look through the papers. I just slide it shut and go to the bottom drawer, pulling it open with a deep breath.

Kyle Kincade

I sit down cross-legged and flip through the papers. There are maps of the route he takes to work, the inside of his house, and the inside of the restaurants he frequents. There's even a picture of a car engine which I assume must be his. There's his schedule for each day of the week. There's his personal information - name, birth date, even social security number. I flip faster. None of this is helping me escape. And I need to escape. I need to warn Kyle.

If it isn't already too late.

I pause for a moment when I see my name. I shiver as I draw the folder out. In angry red marker on the front is written, Amy-Kate Hillsdale. I shudder. Inside is information about me. Lots of information about me. My vision goes a little tipsy. I mean, I know she kidnapped me. But seeing all her research and meticulous notes about my life is disturbing. And then there are the photos. Lots of photos. Of me. Just me. Walking into work. Leaving the coffee shop. Talking on my phone. Even one from the outside taken through the window at mom's flower shop as I'm arranging the wedding bouquet. Apparently, she's been following me for weeks. How long has she been planning to kidnap me?

I feel sick. I was being followed. I was being stalked. In the creepiest way.

I need to get all this to the police. I debate for a moment, then stick the file in the waistband of my pants, against my back. I'm getting out, and this folder is coming with me. I go to close the Kyle drawer when I see a folder labeled Ex-Girlfriends. I realize I am in a life or death situation, but my curiosity gets the better of me. I pull the folder out. Inside are the kinds of things I am coming to except of Amanda's stalking. It looks like Kyle has had several serious girlfriends, as well as a dozen or so flings. And every single one of them is in here. There are photos of each of the girls, and oddly a few of them look a lot like Jillian. There are personality profiles on them. And through it all are Amanda's hand-written notes.

Blond hair

Southern accent?

Seems to prefer needy women

She's analyzing these girls. Gleaning what she can about what Kyle found attractive in a woman so she could waltz in and sweep him of his feet, take all his money, and leave him dead.

I set the folder on top of the folder about me and get to my feet.

It's time to escape.

The question is, how on earth am I going to do that?

# Chapter Thirty-Seven

I GO BACK TO THE DOOR and glare at it, like that's going to help. I need to be clever. More clever than Amanda. The problem is, I don't even watch crime shows or read mysteries or anything. This is very much beyond me. Where is Rachelle when I need her?

I look around the room. I'm in a basement, I am pretty sure. So underground. There is no way I'm going to tunnel through the cement walls and then up through the ground with nothing more than my fingernails and a filing cabinet key. So the door really seems the only option. I don't know how to pick locks, and I don't have a lock pick set or a bobby pin or anything like that on me to try and figure it out.

I look down at myself, assessing my outfit to see if it can be of any help. Jeans. Hoodie. T-shirt. The shoelaces were helpful. Could they be helpful again? Socks. Shoes. One elastic keeping my hair up. I don't think any of that will be of help.

I look at the door again. If I can't get through the locks, how else can I get through? Blast it open? Kick it down? I step back and then run at the door, giving a flying kick to it. I bounce off and lose my balance, toppling to the floor with an, "Oof!" The door is unharmed. Don't think that's going to work, I think as I get to my feet and dust myself off.

It's a wooden door. Could I burn it down? I don't have anything to start a fire with though.

Then I see the hinges. They're on this side of the door. Three of them - top, middle, and bottom. If I get rid of the hinges, would it open even though it's locked?

It's definitely worth a try. I get closer to the hinges and examine them. I don't have much to work with, but this seems my best option. I try pulling the pins that hold the hinges together out with my hands, but they don't budge. So I go and get the filing cabinet key and wedge the key under the lip of the middle hinge. It takes a minute, but I manage to force it between the top of the pin and the hinge itself, making the pin slide up just a fraction. I grin. It's going to work!

What feels like forever later, I'm still working on the first pin. This is incredibly slow work and my poor fingers feel bruised with all the pushing and tugging and maneuvering of this little key. But the pin is half-way out! I grab it in both hands as well as I can and yank with all my might. After this,

I'm going to be an exercise addict, freaking out about getting kidnapped again and working out every day to be strong enough to break down doors and snap handcuffs in half.

The pin pops free and I fly backwards, hitting my butt on the ground. I let out a whoop. And then slap my hand over my mouth and cower, worried Amanda heard and will come investigate. Nothing happens. I let out my breath slowly and then get to my feet, flexing my sore fingers. One down. Two to go.

The second pin is easy, sliding out quickly without much of a fight. But the third pin, the one on top of the door, is not giving up it's hold at any cost. It doesn't help that I'm short and have to work on it with my hands stretched above my head, the blood draining out of my stiff fingers. I should have done this one first, I realize, when I still had energy and my fingers weren't going numb. The desk is too heavy for me to drag over to stand on, and weirdly there is no chair at the desk. I guess Amanda thought I might be able to use it somehow. She was right. I would love a chair to stand on right now. Maybe I could even bash the door down with it.

I drop my arms and shake them out, trying to get blood back into them. I can do this, I tell myself. Just one more hinge and then I'm free! I've got this!

I can do this, I chant in my head, over and over. I can do this. I reach up and dig the key into the top pin again. I can do this!

It takes so long I'm sure Amanda is going to come back and tie me up again. Or just shoot me. Either one of which I don't think I have the strength to survive at this point.

Slowly, painfully, the pin comes free. When it finally wiggles out that last centimeter, I drop it to the floor and let my arms dangle, exhausted. They tingle as blood rushes back into them. I did it.

Now to see if this actually worked.

Swallowing, I give the door an experimental shove. Nothing happens. Then I shake my head at my silliness. It's braced into the door frame on the other side. I'll have to open it toward me. I pull on the handle, but it's no good. I need to move the other side of the door, where the hinges are. Groaning, I get the little key again and dig it into the space between the door and the frame. I wiggle the door toward me, bit by bit, until my fingers can get a slight hold on it and then I work it toward me. It's moving! I get it far enough out of the frame to get my fingers behind it and then I pull. It opens! It actually opens! Not all the way, but enough. Enough for a small girl to slide through.

I hesitate and peer into the dark hallway beyond. Amanda can't be home, right? Or she would have heard me before now. I hope. But she did have me call Kyle and give him this address. So I don't know why she would leave. Either way, I have to take my chances.

I suck in my breath, slip through the opening, and dart

down the dark hallway. It ends at a staircase that I tiptoe up to a door. I listen at it, but hear nothing.

I turn the knob, praying it's not locked too. It isn't. It opens into a kitchen, dark and silent. There are windows across the room, above the sink, looking out onto a dark empty driveway. She really isn't here. I exhale in relief. Maybe she ran to the store to grab something before committing murder? I have no idea.

I scurry through the kitchen into a living room and then the entryway. The front door is locked, but the great thing about front doors is that they open from the inside. I flip the deadbolt and the little flimsy lock on the knob and I'm free!

I creep outside and then crouch beside the house, feeling for some reason like I'm the criminal. If Amanda comes back and finds me now, she'll shoot me for sure. All my hard work will be for nothing. I need the cops. But I don't have my phone. And pay phones aren't really a thing anymore. Time is ticking. Where can I get a phone? Was there one in Amanda's kitchen? I try to remember. I should have checked, but I was so worried about getting out. And I don't know if I have the courage to go back in there.

I look around. It seems we're in the country. Amanda's house is large and she has a lot of land. The only other house looks like it's a mile down the road. I guess that's convenient for her. No one to hear her victims scream.

My eyes focus on a distant house, Amanda's neighbor.

They would have a phone. Right? Do people still have landlines?

I begin running to the neighbor's house, all crouched over along the bushes at the side of the road like that will make me less noticeable if Amanda shows up. But after a few minutes I have to slow to a jog and then a brisk walk. It is seriously a ways away and I am apparently not in great shape. When I finally reach the house and make it up their very long driveway, I glance around the front porch. The house is dark and there's not even a blue TV light glowing inside. But I ring the doorbell anyway. Then I smooth out my hair and tug on my shirt. I'm sure I look a mess.

No one answers. I ring the bell again, a couple time, and then knock, loudly and insistently. I don't care if they've already gone to bed or even if they have a baby sleeping and I wake her! This is life or death!

There's still no answer. Ugh!

I debate for a moment, leaning over to look through their kitchen window where they have conveniently forgotten to close the curtains. I step closer, aware of how creepy this would look to someone watching, and peer in the window, cupping my hands to look better.

It's hard to see in the dark, but I scan the counter tops and walls, like I'm going to magically see a cell phone lying there. And then I do! Not a cell phone but a corded phone mounted on the wall. I blink in surprise.

They actually have a phone!

I run to the door and knock again as loud as I can, ringing the doorbell insistently. Still no one answers. They must not be home. I look around as if hoping another neighbor is going to sprout up in the countryside, but it's just farm fields.

An idea comes to me. A crazy idea.

Breaking in can't be any harder than breaking out, right?

# Chapter Thirty-Eight

BREAKING AND ENTERING is a crime. But this is an emergency! Kyle's life is in danger and I need a phone. Now! Surely the police will understand. Right?

I take a deep breath, step back, lift my foot, and kick the door, right by the handle, like they do on TV. I get bounced back a little and have to hop to keep my balance. The door is unharmed. Great.

I bite my lip, then sigh and grab a rock. I really, really hope that I don't end up in jail at the end of this. Though, I guess jail is better than dead.

I throw the rock hard at glass pane on the door. It shatters with a crash, the rock landing inside.

I use another rock to clear away the sharp bits of glass still left in the door frame and then reach through and fumble with the door handle on the inside. I find the deadbolt and twist it open with a thud, then press the handle and swing the door open. That was easy. That was almost too easy.

I shudder. People could be breaking in all over the place if they really wanted to. I suspect I will have strong opinions about security systems after this is over. Assuming I get to stay in my own apartment. And that I'm alive. I'm sure the prison has a great security system.

I step inside and close the door quickly behind me. Then I race to find the kitchen phone. The house is nice, like Amanda's. These rich country folks know how to live. Or, retire. I assume it's an old couple from the chair lift installed by the staircase.

Great. I'm robbing a little old lady.

Not robbing. Just borrowing a phone. In an emergency. But I did smash in her window. I wince. I'll pay for the damages when this is over.

I run through a living room that smells like old lady perfume and then into the kitchen, scanning walls and tabletops as I go.

There! The land-line I saw from outside is nestled into it's holder on the wall. Perfect. Maybe it's a good thing this is an old lady's house and not some punk college kid who just has a cell phone.

I grab the receiver just as I hear a man's voice coming from the direction of the front door say loudly, "What the-"

I freeze. That was not a little old lady.

"Go back to the car," the man says to someone. "I'll handle this."

Dang it.

I waver with the receiver in hand, wondering if I should still call and just whisper.

And then I hear the door opening, broken glass crunching underfoot.

"Hi, this is Daniel Smith," the man says, his voice getting louder.

I look for a place to hide, but I can't very well take the corded phone with me! It's stuck to the wall.

"I'd like to report a break in at my grandma's house," the guy - Daniel Smith - says. "Yeah, we just got home and the glass on the door is smashed."

He steps into the kitchen, cell phone to his ear, flicks on the light, and sees me. He stops dead. He's about college age, scrawny and still waiting for his shoulders to fill out. I'm a little surprised he had the guts to venture in here alone. Maybe it's just a lack of common sense. For all he knows, I could be dangerous and armed.

We stare at each other, each holding a phone. Both trying to call the same people.

"The- the robber-" he stammers, backing away. "She's still here!"

I feel like Goldilocks. Well, at least he took care of calling

911 for me. The cops should be here soon.

His face hardens as he takes me in, as if realizing I'm not a threat.

I hold my hands up, the phone still in one of them.

He's still on the call with the cops, but I talk anyway. "Look," I say. "I just needed to use a phone to call the cops. Your next-door neighbor is a crazy serial killer! She kidnapped me and is going to kill my boyfriend. Well, ex-boyfriend, but that's beside the point! I'm just saying, I'm not a robber. I'll pay for the damages. I just need the cops. So, thanks for calling them?"

He's watching me with concern now, like his opinion shifted again from harmless girl after money to escaped asylum patient.

The kitchen window overlooks the driveway and I can see the side of Amanda's house in the distance. I glance at it anxiously, and then do a double take as I realize the lights are on. When did that happen? They weren't on when I left!

I run to the window.

"Don't move," Daniel Smith says.

I ignore him.

Sure enough, there's Amanda's car in the drive. I grit my teeth. Has she already discovered that I've escaped? And then, to my horror, I watch as another car pulls into the drive. I stare open mouthed as Kyle gets out, closes the door, straightens his iconic blue suit coat, and strides up to Amanda's door.

Oh. My. Gosh. He actually came. And Amanda is going to kill him.

I look around the kitchen, but Daniel Smith is blocking the only exit.

"I really have to go!"

He glares at me. "Yeah, I'm still here," he says into the phone. "The girl is maybe late twenties with brown hair." A pause. "Uh, she's a little shorter than me so-"

I stop listening, looking around the kitchen for another escape. But there isn't one. Then my gaze lands on the knife block. I raise my eyebrows. I really am going to end up in jail, I think. I lunge forward and grab a knife.

"I'm really sorry," I say, wielding the knife. Daniel Smith jumps backwards, looking horrified. "But I have to go! I'll explain later! Now, get out of the way!"

He flattens himself against the wall, eyes wide, and I run for the front door. I see the little old lady I expected - his grandma, I assume - waiting in the car's passenger seat as I dash out the front door, sliding a little on broken glass. Her eyes go wide at the sight of me and her kitchen knife, and she clutches her hands to her chest. I really hope I didn't just give his granny a heart attack.

I run down the road and toward Amanda's house, very aware that I look like a crazy lady fleeing the scene of the crime and if the cops pull up right now, they will have no trouble picking me out as the lady they got a call about. No time for regrets.

I run all the way to Amanda's and skid to a halt in front of her front door, panting hard. I try the handle. Locked. Of course. Well, breaking and entering a second time can't do much more damage to my record at this point.

I look around for a rock, and then realize there are none. Amanda's front yard has only perfectly manicured grass and blood red roses.

My palms are sweating. How long will it take her to kill him? If the cops get here quick enough can they rush him to a hospital and save him?

I take a deep breath, and then use the handle of the knife to smash the window. Adrenaline makes me strong. The window shatters. I don't take the time to clear away the shards this time. I just reach through, trying to ignore the bite of the glass on my hands. This is nothing compared to what Amanda is about to do to Kyle.

I grip the handle and open the door.

# Chapter Thirty-Nine

I SPRING INTO THE entryway.

Kyle's shoes are sitting to the side beside Amanda's heels.

I run straight for the living room.

Amanda is standing, frowning, two champagne glasses in her hands. Is she going to poison him?

Kyle is sitting on the couch. He starts to his feet when I burst in.

I barrel straight into Amanda, knocking both of us to the floor. The champagne glasses go flying and smash on the carpet.

Amanda shrieks and lashes out with her nails. I roll away and scramble to my feet ready for a fight, still holding the kitchen knife.

Kyle jumps between us, eyes on the knife.

"Woah!" he says. "Calm down!"

"Don't drink anything she gives you!"

Amanda gets to her feet, tugging on her miniskirt and glaring at me. "She's lying!" she says, pointing a finger at me. "Don't believe anything she says! You heard what she thought about Jillian! She's jealous of everyone and angry that you dumped her!"

"That is so not true!" I say. "Well, okay, maybe I was a little jealous. But-"

The screech of sirens cuts me off. We all turn at the same moment toward the sound. Amanda hisses. Kyle frowns. I drop the knife.

The sirens come to an abrupt halt. A moment later someone bangs on the door. Kyle, bewildered, looks between me and Amanda as we stare each other down. Amanda's look is so familiar. It's the look that made me cringe and shy away from jer in high school, and even at the reunion. A look of utter disgust and contempt. But I am not backing down now.

Kyle goes to the door.

"Don't-" Amanda says, but cuts herself off with a manicured hand to her mouth. Maybe she knows it will make her sound guilty, not wanting the cops here. She glares at me again and then follows Kyle.

I hurry to follow as well, not wanting to be the last one to get my story heard by the cops.

"This is the police!" they shout from the other side of the

door. "We know you're in there! Come out with your hands up!"

Kyle glances over his shoulder at us, eyebrows raised.

The police barge in the moment the door is open, four of them with guns out. Kyle raises his hands and steps back.

"Is everyone all right?" one of the officers asks, looking at the three of us. "We heard there was a break in next door. The man said the robber left his place and he then watched her break in here."

Kyle's eyebrows shoot up and he turns slowly to look at me.

"It's her!" Amanda says, pointing an accusing fingernail at me. "She broke in and threatened us with a knife! She's crazy! You need to lock her up!"

The cops start toward me and I put my hands up, showing that I'm not a threat. I really don't want to get shot by the police after all my hard work to stay alive tonight.

"Amanda is the serial killer that detective has been looking for," I say loudly, nodding my head at Amanda. "The one connected to all the mysterious deaths of CEOs and rich single men."

One of the cop takes my hands and pushes me against the wall, beginning to handcuff me. "You have the right to remain silent!"

"I don't want to remain silent! I've had enough of remaining silent! Listen!" I say. "That woman there kidnapped me tonight! I had to break out of here and find a phone to call the cops - you guys! - to get help. She is a serial killer and is planning to murder Kyle!"

The cop has the handcuffs on me now and I can't see his face with my own face pressed up against Amanda's pale peach wall. But he has paused. I take that as a good sign and keep going.

"I've got proof. I have files in - uh, in the waistband of my pants." Now is not the time for blushing, I tell myself. "I took them from Amanda's basement. If you look in her basement you'll find a whole filing cabinet with stuff about each of the dead men. As well as Kyle!"

"She's lying!" Amanda says. "She's crazy! If there's anything in my basement, she planted it there to frame me. She's just jealous, and she's trying to get rid of me! She broke in here with a knife!"

"Kyle Kincade?" one of the other police men says. "I didn't recognize you at first! What a pleasure!" He holds out his hand, grinning.

"Garrison," barks the first cop, and the second falls silent. "Check her."

My face flames as they lift my shirt and pull the files from the back of my pants. Stupid blush.

I hear them flipping though the files, though I can't see anything with my face still shoved up against the wall.

"She's trying to frame me!" Amanda says. "Don't believe

a word she says!"

"There's more proof in her basement," I say again.

"You can't just barge into my house and search it!" Amanda says. "I have rights!"

The officer still doesn't speak, and I hear more pages being flipped.

"We can't search without probable cause," the officer says. "But these files sure look like probable cause to me."

I exhale in relief.

"Search the place," he says. "I want a sample of both these women's hand writing and I want the basement checked out. Ma'am," he says. "You're going to have to come with us."

I assume he's talking to me, but Amanda shrieks. I turn just enough to see her try to run for it, but an officer lunges forward and catches her, pinning her to the ground and wrestling her into handcuffs. I smile so wide my cheek gets squished into the wall.

"You have the right to remain silent," he says over the sound of Amanda's shrieks.

"You can't do this to me! I'm innocent! That woman is insane!"

I cautiously pull my head away from the wall.

"You'll have to come with us too," he says to me.

I deflate a little, but what did I expect?

They take Amanda away immediately and then lead me to a second cop car, still in handcuffs. Just as I'm ducking my head to get in, another car pulls up. Not a police car, but an beat up old gray Honda with a vinyl decal of a cat in a cardboard box on the back window.

Fred leaps out without even turning off the car and rushes across the lawn to toward me.

"Amy-Kate!" He careens around the side of the police car, almost knocking into the officer escorting me. "It's not her!" he says in a rush. "It's that other woman! I swear on my life! Amy-Kate is innocent! I'll testify in any court!"

"Whoa there, sonny," says the officer, holding up a hand to stop Fred's advance. "If you would like, you can head over to the station to give a statement, but we'll have to ask you not to interfere here."

Fred looks at me, slightly wild-eyed. "Are you all right? Did Amanda hurt you? I was trying to tell you on the phone that the photo looked like Amanda to me, but I didn't tell you in time! I am so sorry!" He looks so concerned, so flustered. It's incredibly adorable and makes my cheeks heat.

"I'm okay," I tell him. "I'm fine. They got Amanda! They're just taking me in for questioning. How did you get here?"

"You sounded so scared on the phone so I called the cops —"

"It'll have to wait," the cop says. "We're taking her in. She's in police custody. Unless you're her lawyer?"

Fred shakes his head and steps back. "I'll see you there," he says. "I'm so glad you're okay."

I smile and blush at the relief in his voice and have to look away before I look like an idiot in front of all these cops.

Kyle, without handcuffs, is getting into another police car. I assume he's going to the station to give a statement. He's white. He doesn't even glance my direction.

"Get in the car, ma'am," the officer says.

"One second," I say, looking at Fred. He's watching the car with Kyle drive away, a crease between his eyebrows. His hair is a disaster, and his eyes, when he looks back at me are bright. I have never seen him look so handsome. He drove out here to save me, I realize. He cared that much. He's always cared. For him, it was never about how I looked or who I was with or how successful I was. He just cared about me.

"There's something I have to do real quick," I say to the officer. "It will only take a moment."

"Ma'am-" the officer begins.

But I've already stepped forward and looped my handcuffed arms over Fred's head.

His eyes go wide and his cheeks go pink.

"Fred?" I ask.

"Uh, yeah?" His voice is a little scratchy.

"My answer is yes. I would love to go on a date with you sometime."

His eyes light up and he opens his mouth to say something, but I don't hear what it is because, blushing like a ripe tomato, I stretch up on my tiptoes, lean forward, and press my lips to the lower lip of his open mouth.

He inhales sharply. Then his mouth closes, his hands come around my waist, and he kisses me back, slow and gentle, like he is in awe.

For a moment, I get lost in him. His mouth is warm and tastes like peppermint. His hands press into the small of my back, cradling me like something precious.

Then the police officer clears his throat. "Ma'am. I need to ask you to step away from this man and get into the car."

Fred jerks back, like the officer startled him. I see his Adam's apple bob as he swallows. "Uh, right," he says. "Um, I guess I should-" He lets go of my waist with one hand and gestures toward his car.

"Yeah," I say, a little breathless. "Right, okay." I lift my arms from around his neck. I'm sure my cheeks are bright red, but I'm grinning. "Rain check?"

He grins too, glancing at the officer and then back at me, maybe a little shyly. "Yeah. I'd like that."

I step back and the officer takes my shoulder, ducking me into the car. Fred watches, hands in his pockets, an almost goofy grin on his face. I wave my bound hands out the back of the car window as we drive away and Fred waves back.

It's going to be a long messy night ahead of me, but if they search Amanda's place, I am positive they'll find enough evidence to convict her. Most importantly, everyone is still alive.

I mouth at Fred, "We did it!"

Between taking down a serial killer and finally figuring out which guy I actually want to be with, I call tonight a win.

# Epilogue

THE BELL OVER THE flower shop door jingles as I push it open.

"Mom?"

She looks up from behind the counter and relief washes over her features.

"Amy-Kate!" She runs to me and wraps me up in a rare hug. I smile and bury my face in her shoulder. Mom pulls back, with her hands on my shoulders and looks me up and down. "You're a wreck."

I laugh.

"With everything on the news," she says, "I didn't know what to believe!"

"I'm okay." I hesitate, not knowing exactly what to tell her. I hop up on the counter and swing my legs. She frowns but doesn't comment.

"What happened?"

I rub my forehead. "It's a long story. Basically, Amanda's oh-so-successful makeup company wasn't as successful as she said it was. All that money? It came from the dead men on the news. She is going to jail. For a long time, I hope."

"And you're all right?"

I smile. "I'm all right."

She nods and goes over to some flowers, drawing them out of their vase of water. Grabbing the shears, she starts snipping off leaves.

Maybe I'll tell Mom the details later, but honestly, she probably doesn't want to know.

Amanda has been charged with five counts of first degree murder, one attempted murder, and one kidnapping - mine. Facial recognition software is analyzing the one grainy photo of the serial killer fiance and I am positive it will come back as a match for Amanda. She's locked in jail without bail and waiting her trial. Kyle and I are both going to testify at it. Not looking forward to that.

I got off with nothing more than a fine to pay for the damages I caused the Smith house. But those are on hold until Amanda is tried for my kidnapping. If she's convicted, she'll have to pay. Which, it turns out, will be difficult. Even with all the money she's stolen from five dead guys, somehow it appears she has some serious credit card debt. In the meantime, a victim assistance fund is paying to replace the Smith's window.

I stopped by their house on the way home to apologize in person, and Granny Smith, as I call her in my head, said she owes me her life and not to worry. I feel like that's an exaggeration since Amanda was going after single rich men, not old ladies, but whatever. Granny Smith made me a tall pitcher of lemonade and a batch of snicker doodle cookies, and we sat and talked on her back porch. She's the nicest old lady I've ever met and said if I needed an extra grandma that she would adopt me. Her grandson, Daniel, who lives in her basement while attending university, was more reluctant about forgiving me, but admitted that they're grateful they no longer have a serial killer for a neighbor.

All in all, it's been an exhausting past 24 hours, but I couldn't be happier.

"I've been thinking," I say. "About what you asked earlier. About you retiring and handing over the flower shop to me."

Mom nods. "I know. You said you don't want it. I've found a couple of interested people, but I'm thinking I'll wait a little longer. None of them seem quite right."

"I changed my mind," I say.

Mom stops fiddling with the flowers and looks at me. "You did?"

I nod. "I did. I want the flower shop. In fact, I would love the flower shop! I was just scared to accept it because I didn't think I'd do a good job running it, but-" I'm not sure how to explain without totally freaking her out. Now that I've dated one of the most famous men in the world, escaped a kidnapping, single handedly taken down a serial killer, and finally stood up to Amanda, I feel a lot more capable. "I think I can handle the flower shop," I say aloud.

Mom shakes her head. "You are so silly, Amy-Kate. Of course you can handle the flower shop. You grew up here! You know this place better than anyone else! You've seen me run it your whole life. If you can't run this place, no one can! You could run this place with both hands tied behind your back!"

I snort. "Don't say that." Then I smile. "In fact, I found out about this little space for rent downtown and I was thinking about expanding the flower shop and opening up a second location."

Mom's eyes widen. "That might actually be a good idea. We've been getting a lot more orders lately, almost too many to handle, but if we had a second location that could speed things up a lot. We could handle a lot more orders that way."

I grin. "Exactly. And it's near a little coffee shop that has been getting a lot of attention. I think that part of town is about to become really popular."

My phone vibrates in my pocket. When I dig it out, I see Kyle's name. I hesitate a second.

"I've got to take this," I tell Mom, jumping off the counter and pushing into the back room of the shop.

"Hey," I say.

"Hello." His voice is husky.

A beat of silence.

"Are you all right?" he asks.

"Yeah, you?"

"Yes, thank you for inquiring."

I laugh a little at his formal language.

"Amy-Kate," he says. "I made a terrible mistake breaking up with you. I am so sorry. Can you forgive me?"

I swallow. "It's all right, Kyle," I say. "No hard feelings."

"Thank you."

Another beat of silence.

"Amy-Kate, I would like it very much if you would consent to be my girlfriend again."

I suck in my breath. He wants me to be his girlfriend again? Actually, of course he wants me! I'm awesome! I escaped from a serial killer! I saved his life! Any guy would fall for me after that!

But… I think of Fred. Fred with his easy grin, cheesy science-pun t-shirts, and simple confidence in me. Not to mention his lips...

Then I think of how handsome Kyle is. I think of the presents he buys me. I think of how people see me when I'm with him. I like all of that.

But I also think of the fancy restaurants with strange food. I think of how uncomfortable the dresses and heels are, even though I did look good in them. I think of how I tried to change myself to match Kyle. That wasn't me. I'm the kind of girl who likes hoodies and converse. I like comfort food and bad puns. I like pizza and board games, I realize, a lot more than I like fancy lunches on private yachts.

I don't need to be Amanda to be successful. I don't need to change anything. I don't even need a rich, handsome, famous boyfriend. I am enough just the way I am.

"Actually," I say. "I'm really flattered you want to date me, but I'm no longer interested. Good luck with everything." And then I hang up the phone.

I'm surprised to find that I am smiling.

I don't need a boyfriend. But I really do like hanging out with one guy in particular. One guy who I can be myself around. One guy who saw my potential before I did.

I call up Fred.

"Amy-Kate!" he says. "I tried to get into the police station to see you, but it was swarmed with reporters, and the police said I couldn't see you unless I'm your attorney. Where are you? Are you okay?"

I laugh. "Yeah, I'm good. I'm great actually!"

"Oh good." I hear the relief in his voice and it warms me. "I was worried. What you did was amazing though! I knew you could rock the world! And now look at you, literally saving people's lives!"

I laugh. "I was actually calling to say how awesome you

are," I say.

"Wait, what?"

"Thanks for believeing in me, Fred," I say. "It means a lot to me."

I can practically hear the embarassment in his voice as he says, "It was nothing. You're easy to believe in."

I smile, blushing, of course. "So, how about that date?"

# Acknowledgments

Thank you to everyone who helped make this book possible! Thank you to my husband, Alex, who supports me as a writer, both financially while I am starting out and emotionally when I feel inadaquate. Thank you to my Mom for being my main editor and coming up with awesome ideas for this book! It would have been way less exciting without your input. Thank you to my launch team for looking for typos and helping spread the word, especially Crystal Nelson, Shaun Phipps, and Kristine Leach. And thank you to all the authors who wrote so many books for me to read growing up. The world is a better place with good books in it!

# About the Author

IZI MILLER has a Bachelor's degree in English from Brigham Young University and a Masters of Library and Information Science from Valdosta State University. She and her adorably nerdy husband live in Idaho with their black cats, Cinder and Nico. Her favorite flowers are pink daisies. She loves succulents, cat-pun t-shirts, and making tissue paper flowers.

www.izimiller.com
izimillerauthor@gmail.com

# The Sweet Suspense Series

MY VERY OWN HITMAN is the first book in this Sweet Suspense series! Don't miss it!

Alex is Jessica's type of guy - handsome, rich, and surprisingly nice. Oh, and he's also a hitman sent to kill her. Minor details.

Keep reading for a sneak peak at the first chapter!

# My Very Own Hitman

## Chapter One

I SLIP ON THE ICE, my foot skittering out from under me, my knee coming down hard on the pavement, and when the package I'm holding hits the ground, I just about have a heart attack.

I hold my breath, waiting for the explosion.

But…

Nothing happens.

I stare at the package. It doesn't blow up.

I let out my breath.

Wincing, I get up. My skinny jeans have a new hole in the knee. I shove my hair out of my face, then gather the brown paper package back into my arms and wrap my coat around it. I imagine myself hunkered down, a brave soldier protecting civilians from its grenade-like force. But in reality, my nerves are frayed like the end of a stripped wire.

Exhaling visible air, I shiver and slide my shoes over the ice so I will not slip again. The need to hurry is a physical grip tightening around my lungs. As if the timer is already ticking down on the explosives. I know it's ticking down on D's temper.

It's occurred to me several months ago that if D ever wanted me gone, he could time the explosives to go off while I carry them. I never open the packages. If I did and he found out, I wouldn't need a detonator to be done for. I only feel the bulk of each package beneath my fingers - different shapes, sizes, weights.

Once, a package was ticking under my fingers, the noise so staccato it might have been able to stab me with the sound alone. I was sure my heart was going to explode in my chest before it had a chance to count down to zero, but I handed it off without anything happening.

To me at least.

I don't know how the explosives work or what they're for. I've seen D open them though. I don't know what he does with them, and I don't want to know. I heard one of his guys say something about shipping supplies to Venezuela once, so maybe he's sending things there. Then again, there was that explosion near the state capitol last year, right after he'd had me bring in a whole herd of packages from some fertilizer shop out in cow country miles from the city. I very much did not want to know if D had anything to do with that.

Although I don't know what happens to the bigger packages, I've seen him take the smaller packages into the back room. At first, I thought they were explosives too. But those packages apparently contain guns. D occasionally lets me see what he does with them, and with people who stop cooperating. I've seen guys and girls dragged in, and heard the screaming stop when the guns go off.

Sometimes the screaming doesn't stop for a long, long time. Those sessions are reserved for D's "special guests." The ones who try to run.

D thinks it's good for me to have a glimpse of what he does. He says it keeps me in line.

He's right. I never want to be the one screaming through my gag in that back room.

I shouldn't be out here, I think. I should be sipping cocoa and cuddling with a boy while we watch sappy chick flicks or something. I'm a single college student for goodness sake! With my long light brown hair, pretty nose and green eyes, I'm not all that bad looking either. If it weren't for the dark circles under my eyes and the way my clothes get looser every month, I'd be quite a catch. I should be going ice skating with someone handsome and then kissing him under mistletoe.

As it is, the only guys I get to hang out with these days aren't exactly the kind who would make me cocoa.

Unless it had arsenic in it.

I'm freezing my fingers off. Alone. Too bad I cut the fingertips off my gloves. It makes texting easier, but when the cold makes my hands stiff, texting is agonizing anyway.

New gloves are at the top of things I want and will not be getting for Christmas. Not the cheap dollar store kind that don't hold any heat, but thick warm ones that don't get soaked every time I pick up a handful of snow.

Actually, what I really wish is that I was getting paid to deliver these packages, in a regular job with the Post Office or UPS, instead of getting blackmailed to jump at D's beck and call. I wish I didn't have to skip class, call in sick to work, and run on five hours of sleep a night just to stay alive.

I know it's stupid, but while I'm wishing, I might as well wish for a boyfriend. All of it is equally impossible.

Of course, one guy has my number.

I'll be in class or asleep in the middle of the night or at the grocery store checking ramen prices when I get a text. All it will have is an address, and I know I have to go.

One time my cell chimed in the middle of a history

exam, while I was writing a 250 word essay on how Napoleon influenced Western art, and I stood up, walked across the testing center, and handed in my exam, less than half done, knowing I would get an F.

The phone number is always different and the addresses are always different, but it always means the same thing. A pick up. Sometimes the addresses are in back alleys or sketchy bars where a guy dressed all in black hands me a package. Sometimes D himself meets me.

They're not always explosives and guns. I've carried around drugs and even pieces of disassembled weapons or ammo. They'd never give me something I could actually use to defend myself—like a loaded weapon.

Sometimes it's just a letter. Probably blackmail for some other unfortunate soul D's tangled with. Sometimes it's a message, not even written down, that I have to repeat back to D word for word before he'll let me go and deliver it. The messages never make any sense to me.

At least I haven't been forced to hide a body.

Yet.

I get to the apartment complex and duck between two buildings. The place is run-down and forgotten. A string of broken Christmas lights blinks on and off in a window across the street. The side of one building has crumbled away like someone started a demolition project and then gave it up. Rusty cars are parked across faded yellow lines like this lot is a graveyard for abandoned vehicles.

The nearest street light burned out over a year and a half ago, a few months after I started working with D, and other than the blinking Christmas lights, the parking lot is dark now, making the ice black. I hold the explosives closer, like they need protecting.

I feel my way down the three concrete stairs to the bottom apartment level where the windows peek halfway over the asphalt of the parking lot like suspicious eyes. A paper pasted on one of the apartment doors announces that the place has been condemned.

I stop in front of the fourth door on the right. No number. Just a slash across the roughed-up wood, like someone got in a knife fight right up next to it. It should be 7 since doors 6 and 8 flank it. But in my mind, I think of it as Apartment Zero.

This apartment should be nothing. It should be burned to the ground, decimated with a wrecking ball, and blown up into trillions of particles. It should be non-existent. Erased. Blipped off the map.

It should be nothing. And yet it is everything. This apartment is my life.

I rap my knuckles on the wood. Tap-tap. Tap. My hand is shivering in the cold, so the taps come out wrong. Too soft. Off rhythm. I blow on my fist, cradling the package in one arm like a baby. It's so rectangular. I'm used to lumpier things. It feels strange. Normal. Like it could be school books. I almost smile at the thought.

I knock again, louder this time, and get the rhythm right. Tap-tap-tap. Tap.

I wait, glancing over my shoulder.

No one answers my knock. I know I'm late, but not that late. Fifteen minutes at the most. Someone should be here to collect. Maybe my messed-up tapping threw them off.

I knock again. Tap-tap-tap. Tap.

When no one answers, I hoist the box up higher in my arm, almost tucking it into my armpit. Then I scurry back up the three stairs and head around the building. Someone is always here to pick up deliveries, so if no one is answering there must be something going on in the other room.

The apartment backs onto a narrow alley where dumpsters are lined up like a stinky parade. I ease my foot down gently with each step onto the gravel, trying to make myself silent. There's one window on this side that leads into Apartment Zero, and it's all blacked out with dark paint. Someone chipped away at the paint in one corner, making a tiny crooked smiley face.

I un-focus my eyes so that the smiley face smears in my vision. Then I crouch down and listen. This is the window to the back room. The room I don't want to ever be allowed into.

I hold my breath and lean close to the glass, so close I'm almost touching it. I cup my hand over my mouth and exhale, not letting my breath onto the glass. They couldn't see it through the paint, but I'm paranoid just the same. I have to be.

I hear a low murmur of voices, and I close my eyes like it will help my hearing sharpen. I can make out the rise and fall of words. Sentences. D says something. I recognize his voice, but not the words.

Until I hear my name.

Jessica.

Shocked, I lose my balance and almost bang into the window. I didn't know he knew my name. I've only heard him refer to me as "girl," "you," or "that one."

I place my fingers on the bricks next to the window, and ease myself closer, my breath trapped in my chest. I lean toward the window until there's only a millimeter of air between me and it. I still can't hear everything, so I let my ear press against the cold glass.

"...been dead for a few months now," D is saying. "We don't have anything but threats left."

Someone grunts, low in his throat. Maybe it's a word. I can't tell.

"It's too much hassle to keep her in check. She's never been fully on board. Got to get rid of her before she runs."

I draw in my breath. This is what I have been dreading. I knew this would happen. I've known it for the past two years.

They're going to kill me.

Scan the QR code below to get it on Amazon!